UNFAIR ODDS

Clint decided that Billy London was going to have to handle Lonnie Cord all by himself. He was going to keep his eyes on the three miners at the bar.

"You gonna come up with my money, gambler?" Cord shouted.

London just stared at the man.

"Damn you—" Cord shouted and drew his gun.

Clint heard the report of the derringer, which he thought came from London's sleeve, but then he was looking at the men at the bar. All three of them drew their guns and Clint stood up shouting, "Don't!"

His shout distracted them for just a second, but that was long enough. By the time they decided to go ahead and fire at London, Clint was pulling the trigger on his own gun. There was no time for anything fancy so he just pumped a bullet into the thickest part of each man.

"Jesus—" he heard somebody say.

The three miners at the bar never got off a shot . . .

111 W. 4th
Pratt, KS 67124
Phone (316) 672-9507

DON'T MISS THESE
ALL-ACTION WESTERN SERIES
FROM THE BERKLEY PUBLISHING GROUP

THE GUNSMITH by J. R. Roberts
Clint Adams was a legend among lawmen, outlaws, and ladies. They called him . . . the Gunsmith.

LONGARM by Tabor Evans
The popular long-running series about U.S. Deputy Marshal Long—his life, his loves, his fight for justice.

SLOCUM by Jake Logan
Today's longest-running action Western. John Slocum rides a deadly trail of hot blood and cold steel.

McMASTERS by Lee Morgan
The blazing new series from the creators of *Longarm*. When McMasters shoots, he shoots to kill. To his enemies, he is the most dangerous man they have ever known.

THE GUNSMITH

167

CHINAVILLE

J. R. ROBERTS

ROUNDTOP
BOOK SHOP

MONDAY - FRIDAY: 10:00 A.M. - 6:00 P.M.

606 W. Kansas
Greensburg, KS 67054

Kathy Zook
Owner

JOVE BOOKS, NEW YORK

CHINAVILLE

A Jove Book / published by arrangement with
the author

PRINTING HISTORY
Jove edition / November 1995

ISBN: 0-515-11747-1

A JOVE BOOK®
Jove Books are published by The Berkley Publishing Group,
200 Madison Avenue, New York, New York 10016.
JOVE and the "J" design are trademarks
belonging to Jove Publications, Inc.

PRINTED IN THE UNITED STATES OF AMERICA

10 9 8 7 6 5 4 3 2 1

PROLOGUE

Once Virgil Train had made his way in this world with a gun. He had thought nothing of ending a man's life for money. Being fast and deadly with a gun—any kind of gun—was his only talent, and he put it to good use, until the day a little girl got between his bullet and his target. He tried to stop, but he couldn't, and the little girl was killed. His opponent's bullet struck him in the chest, and when he woke up he was looking into the face of a man wearing a white clerical collar.

"Father?" he asked.

"I am a minister."

"The little girl?"

"She's dead, I'm afraid," the minister said. "She died instantly, if that is of any consolation."

"It isn't," Train said, frowning. It did not even occur to him to ask about the other man. His remorse was instantaneous, and almost unbearable. He had killed a little girl, an innocent child.

Actually, never having experienced the emotion before, Train had to explain to the minister what he was feeling, and the man told him that it was remorse.

"Why did I live," he asked, "and the little girl die?"

"Because," the minister explained, "it was the will of God."

"But why?" Train asked. "Why didn't God let her live and take me?"

"It was her time," the man said, "and not yours."

"I don't understand."

"Apparently," the minister said, "there are still things that you must do."

"Like what?"

"What do you do now?"

"I kill people."

"Well," the minister said firmly, "not that."

"Then what?"

"Perhaps just the opposite," the minister said. "Perhaps you are now meant to save people."

"How would I do that?"

"By helping them to find God."

"But . . . I don't believe in God."

The minister smiled, stood up, and said, "Oh, I think you do . . . now." He left the room.

Left to ponder it, Virgil Train decided that God did indeed exist and had chosen to spare him, otherwise how could he have survived a wound that the doctor later said should have killed him?

In that moment, Virgil Train became the man called "Preach."

ONE

When Clint Adams rode into Chinaville, Colorado, he found it to be just what he was looking for. The town and its surrounding area were the site of recent gold strikes. In fact, the nearby Cripple Creek field was the center of the strike. Because of the size of the strike, Chinaville had benefited—or suffered, depending on one's viewpoint—from an influx of businessmen, working ladies, miners, gamblers, gunmen, saloons, and gambling establishments.

Clint was looking forward to some time spent gambling, primarily at a poker table. Poker relaxed him, and he was looking forward to spending some time relaxing.

The town had formerly been the site of just a few clapboard buildings but, since the strike, more hastily erected buildings had sprung up, as well as tents. Some of the places—like a couple of the saloons— were a combination of wood and tent. The livery stable, however, was wood, and had probably been the first building ever erected there.

"Welcome to Chinaville, stranger," the liveryman said, coming out to meet Clint. "Passin' through or lookin' for a claim?"

"Passing through," Clint said, dismounting. "Panning or mining for gold is not my game."

"What is?" the man asked.

"Like I said," Clint replied, handing the man the reins, "I'm just passing through."

He did not want to tell the man that he had come there looking for poker. The word would surely have gotten around. He wanted a chance to take some gold nuggets off a few miners in a poker game before they realized that was what he was there to do.

He took his rifle and saddlebags from Duke's saddle and then fixed the liveryman with a hard stare.

"You take good care of this horse," he said firmly, patting the big, black gelding's neck.

"Mister, a horse like this deserves the best care in the world, and that's what he's gonna get. I swear."

"I'm going to hold you to that, friend. Where's the nearest hotel?"

"You probably passed it on the way in. It don't say 'hotel' on it, but it's the Buckhorn Saloon. They got rooms upstairs."

"Thanks."

"They got girls, too," the man said, "real pretty ones."

It was then Clint realized how young the man was, probably in his early twenties. His face was filthy enough to hide his age, but now his teeth and the whites of his eyes were showing.

"I'll check them out," Clint said. "Thanks."

"Sure."

It was about one in the afternoon and the town seemed half asleep. That's because the miners were working their claims. Later in the evening they'd come into town, looking to spend what little gold they'd managed to coax out of the ground. Maybe somebody would hit a big strike and come into some saloon to buy drinks for the house. Either way, some of that gold would certainly end up on a poker table.

Clint was in Chinaville because of a bet. He'd been talking with his friend Rick Hartman one day in Hartman's saloon, Rick's Place, in Labyrinth, Texas, when the subject came up of making a living playing poker. . . .

"It's not an easy thing to do," Hartman said. "I managed to do it for quite a few years, but you've really got to be good at the game to make it."

"I could make it," Clint said.

Hartman laughed.

"What's funny?"

"I don't think you could make it, Clint."

"Why not?"

"Oh, your game is almost good enough, but you'd have too much trouble really keeping your mind on it."

"Why is that?"

"Because you get too involved."

They'd had many discussions before about Clint's tendency to become involved with other people's problems, and more than a few arguments—some of which resulted in bets being made.

"What do you mean my game is *almost* good enough?" Clint asked.

"You can hold your own, Clint," Hartman said. "I'm not impugning your game."

"Then what are you saying? What does 'almost good enough' mean?"

"You need to spend more time at the table, is all," Hartman said.

"And what about you? You could go right out and make a living doing it?"

"Well, of course," Hartman said. "After all, I'm a gambler and you're not. That's the difference."

"I say I can go out and make a living as a gambler, Rick," Clint said. "How much do you want to bet?"

"You want to *bet* me on this?"

"That's right."

"Why?"

"Because," Clint said, with a shrug, "at the moment I don't have anything better to do. . . . "

The amount of the bet really didn't matter. All that mattered was that Clint was supposed to return to Labyrinth after a month with the money he'd made playing poker.

Clint had heard some time ago about the strike that had been made in Cripple Creek and Chinaville, and it made sense for him to ride straight for the gold strike to make his "fortune," rather than just drifting from town to town looking for games. He had also considered San Francisco, but if Colorado had a real honest-to-God gold strike it seemed the logical place to go.

Now he entered the Buckhorn Saloon, looked around, and saw a hotel desk across the room from the bar. As he headed for it, the bartender came around from behind the bar and followed. Apparently he was doing double duty. At the moment there were only a few men standing at the bar, and four or five sitting at tables alone. Clint saw three men playing solitaire; he knew they were gamblers waiting for the miners to come to town.

"Help ya?" the man asked, once he got behind the desk.

"I need a room."

"Can't help ya."

"Why not?"

"Hey," the man said, spreading his hands, "this is a mining town, my friend. Rooms are hard to come by."

"Is there anyplace else I can try?" Clint was starting to wish he'd brought his wagon with him. At least he would have been able to sleep inside of it.

"There are plenty of tents on the outskirts of town that will rent you a space—"

"I don't think I want to do that." He figured to be in Chinaville for a while and didn't want to have to spend his nights in a tent, no matter how large or small the space might be.

The man had a heavy black beard that hid his age well, and now he rubbed it with a scarred hand.

"Well, there is one other thing you could try."

"What's that?"

He leaned forward, as if he was about to impart some great secret. Clint leaned forward, so he'd be sure to hear it.

"Lots of things happen around here at night."

"Like what?"

"Men gamble, drink, they get into fights... sometimes there's gunplay."

Clint immediately saw what the man was getting at.

"Are you suggesting I wait around to see if anyone gets killed tonight, and then take their room?"

"That's what I'm suggesting," the man said. "Like I said, it's just something else for you to think about."

Clint thought about it for a long moment and then asked, "Have you got someplace I can put my stuff until then?"

"Sure, friend," the bartender said. "What's your name?"

"Adams," Clint said, "Clint Adams."

The bartender's eyes widened, a sure sign that he recognized the name.

"Mr. Adams," he said, "uh, sure, uh, my name's Vince, Mr. Adams, and I'll take good care of your stuff, and somehow I'll find a room for you."

"I'll just wait, like you said, Vince. Meanwhile, I could use a beer."

"Comin' up, Mr. Adams," Vince said, "comin' right up."

TWO

The bartender took Clint's gear and stowed it away somewhere, then met him at the bar and gave him the first beer on the house.

"Can I get something to eat from you?" Clint asked over the beer.

"Just about anything you want. I got a big kitchen in the back, and a couple of cooks. A steak be good enough for ya?"

"A steak would be fine," Clint said.

"Get yourself a table. I'll bring it out to you when it's done."

"Not *too* done," Clint said.

"Gotcha," the bartender said.

Clint took his beer, turned, and surveyed the room. One or two of the gamblers looked up at him hopefully, but he ignored them and continued scanning with his eyes until he found a table he liked. It was in the rear corner, and he'd be able to sit with his back to the wall.

He was just settling into his chair when one of the gamblers came ambling over, doing one-handed cuts with a deck of cards. He was tall and slender, with dark hair slicked back from a high forehead. He was wearing a boiled white shirt and black pants, and had left his black suit jacket on the back of his chair.

"Afternoon, friend," the man said.

"Afternoon."

"Mind if I join you?"

"I don't see why not."

"Thanks."

The gambler sat across from Clint and smiled broadly. Clint felt the way a fish must feel when he knows the fisherman is baiting the hook for him. The man set the deck on the table and continued to cut.

"My name's Alex Bennett."

"Call me Clint."

"Just get into town, Clint?"

"That's right."

"Plan on stayin' awhile?"

"Maybe."

"Helluva strike up here," Bennett said, shaking his head. "Lots of gold."

"That's good."

"That's mighty good," Bennett said, "especially in my line of work."

"Taken a lot of gold off of miners at the table?" Clint asked.

"Some," Bennett said, cutting over and over again. He leaned forward conspiratorially. "I'm not the only gambler working these miners, you see."

"Really?" Clint was willing to bet that the man was the only gambler using this particular tactic, first making friends with his mark before taking their poke.

"It's dog-eat-dog here, Clint."

"I can imagine."

"Say," Bennett said, sitting back in his chair, "you wouldn't be interested in a friendly game, would you?"

"I might, Bennett," Clint said, "I might, maybe later. Right now I see Vince coming with my steak."

Bennett turned and saw Vince coming toward them carrying a steaming plate of food.

"Well, I'll leave you to your dinner, then," Bennett said, standing up. "Perhaps we can have that friendly game later."

"Sure," Clint said, "later."

"Here ya go, Mr. Adams," Vince said, bustling over to the table and setting the plate down.

Clint saw Bennett stop short as he was walking away and was sure that the gambler had heard his last name.

"Can I get ya another beer?" Vince asked.

"Another beer would be fine, Vince."

"Comin' up."

As Vince headed back to the bar, Bennett, who had reached his own table, grabbed his arm.

"Did you say that man's name was Adams?"

"That's right."

"Clint Adams?"

"Right again," Vince said. "You been tryin' to hustle the Gunsmith into a game, Bennett."

Sweat popped out on Bennett's brow and the gambler said, "Jesus."

THREE

The steak and vegetables went down real easy, and Clint had to insist on paying, as Vince wanted to give it to him for free.

Alex Bennett sat at his table playing solitaire, studiously avoiding looking Clint's way, which was just as well. He hadn't gone to any of the other tables to pass the word that Clint Adams was in town, and after Clint finished eating he decided to make sure that the gambler didn't decide to do just that later.

Clint carried his third beer over to Bennett's table and asked, "Mind if I join you?"

Bennett looked up at him nervously and said, "Huh? Uh, no, not at all. Uh, please do."

As Clint sat Bennett was attempting a one-handed cut and the deck leapt from his hand and spread out on the table.

"What are you so nervous about, Bennett?" Clint asked.

"Well, uh—" Bennett said, gathering the cards up, "I, uh, wouldn't want you to think I was, uh, tryin' to, uh, ya know—"

"Con me into a 'friendly' game of poker?"

Bennett smiled weakly and said, "Oh, uh, yeah, uh, that . . ."

"Now that you know who I am," Clint said, "does that mean you don't want to play poker with me anymore?"

"Well . . . uh, no, it don't mean that at all," Bennett said. "As a matter of fact, I'd be honored to play with you, but, uh, not here—"

"You're more concerned with the easy pickings here, huh?"

"Well, that's why I came here," Bennett said.

"And these other gamblers?"

"Sure, them, too." Suddenly, Bennett looked more closely at Clint. "Say, why are *you* here?"

"Me? I'm just passing through, Bennett."

"But you wouldn't mind getting into a game or two while you're here, is that right?"

"Well . . . I'm always up for a game of poker, Bennett."

"I thought so."

"But," Clint said, leaning forward, "I wouldn't want you passing the word about who I am just yet. Understand?"

Bennett stared at Clint for a moment, then said, "Oh, hey, I wouldn't tell anybody, Mr. Adams. You can count on me."

"I hope so, Bennett, I really hope so. I don't like having my name telegraphed around."

"You can count on me," Bennett said again. "What about, uh, Vince, the bartender?"

"I'll be talking to Vince about this, too, Bennett, don't worry."

"I'm not worried," Bennett said, too quickly. "Will you, uh, be playing at my table or one of the others?"

"I don't know," Clint said. "I'll have to take a look around first."

"Maybe," Bennett said hurriedly, "maybe it would help if I filled you in on who the others are?"

Clint started to say no, then thought better of it. He thought Bennett was too nervous to lie to him, and it might save him some time checking the other men out himself.

"All right," he said. "Fill me in . . . but wait until I talk to Vince."

"Sure."

Clint stood up and asked, "Would you like a beer, Bennett?"

"Uh, me? Oh, sure, yeah, that'd be great."

"Comin' up," Clint said. He started away from the table, then turned back and looked at Bennett.

"Don't go away."

"I'm, uh, not goin' nowhere, I swear."

He went up to the bar and ordered two beers. When Vince brought them, Clint motioned for him to wait a minute.

"Vince, there's something I'd like to get straight with you."

"What's that, Mr. Adams?"

"That," Clint said. "Don't call me by my last name.

I'm not ready for everybody here to know who I am. You've already fixed it so that Bennett knows."

"Gee, I'm sorry, Mr.—uh, what do I call you?"

"Just call me Clint."

"All right . . . Clint."

"And if word gets out about who I am," Clint added, "I'll know it was either you or Bennett. Do you understand?"

"Sure, I understand," Vince said, and then just to prove it added, "Clint."

"Okay," Clint said. He took the two beers and walked back to Bennett's table.

"Thanks," Bennett said as Clint put a beer down by his arm.

Clint sat down with his own beer and said, "Okay, talk."

FOUR

"The fella right behind us and to our right is Patch Brighton."

Clint stole a look at the man, who seemed to have two good eyes.

"Why do they call him Patch?" Clint asked. "He's not wearing one."

Bennett shrugged.

"I don't know. I guess you'll have to ask him . . . I mean, if that's all right, uh, with you—"

"Just go on, Bennett," Clint said. "Is he any good?"

Clint knew this question was subjective. The answer would depend on how good Bennett himself was, but he asked it anyway.

"He's competent."

"And what are you?"

"I'm, uh, very good . . ."

"Really?"

Bennett looked insulted and said, "Yes, really."

"All right, don't get your feelings hurt," Clint said. "Who's the other man, sitting further back?"

"That's Billy London."

Now it was Clint's turn to widen his eyes.

"*The* Billy London?"

"That's right."

"What's he doing playing a mining town?" Clint asked. "I thought he only played the big games in New York, San Francisco, even abroad."

"Billy's fallen on hard times and is tryin' to build himself a stake," Bennett said.

Clint had heard of Billy London for years. It was said that he and Luke Short once played in a big winner-take-all game and finally whittled the game down to the two of them. After forty-eight hours the game had to be called a draw and both players walked away with money. Of all the men Clint had played poker with—Bat Masterson, Ben Thompson, Doc Holliday—Luke Short was the best he'd ever seen. If Billy London was that good, Clint had a problem. To win his bet he'd probably have to stay away from London's table, but he would truly love to play him.

"How do you rate Billy London, Bennett?" Clint asked.

Bennett's answer would go a long way toward establishing his credibility. If he said London wasn't any good, Clint would know not to trust the man's judgment.

"Billy London?" Bennett asked. "Well, Jesus, Clint, he's just about the best there is. Some nights I just stand there and watch him."

"Have you played against him?"

"I have."

"How many times?"

"Three." Bennett answered without hesitation.

"And how did you do?"

"I walked away a loser all three times."

"At least you're honest about it."

"Why wouldn't I be?" Bennett asked. "At least I got to play with the best three times." Suddenly a look of interest crossed Bennett's face. "Say, you've played with some of the best, haven't you?"

"I've been up against some good players."

"You ever play against Luke Short?"

"I have," Clint said. He added proudly, "Luke's a good friend of mine."

"Did you hear about that game him and London had—"

"I heard about it."

"Is that a true story?"

"Far as I know, and I've heard it from Luke."

"God, I'd love to play against Luke Short," Bennett said, "but since I played Billy London, I guess that's almost as good."

"Almost."

"Did they ever play again after that time?" Bennett asked.

"I don't think they ever did."

"Guess it just made sense to stay away from each other, huh?"

"I guess so."

"Who else have you played against, Clint?"

Clint studied Bennett across the table. The man seemed genuinely interested.

"Deal some two-handed stud, Bennett, and we'll talk about it."

FIVE

They talked for a while about who they had played. Bennett had rarely played outside of mining towns or cow towns and an occasional trip into Denver. He was therefore very interested in Clint's stories of places he'd played and people he'd played against, specifically Luke Short and Bat Masterson, who happened to be two of Clint's best friends.

As they talked they played two-handed, just passing dollars back and forth, until a miner came walking in and asked if he could join them. Once the third man entered the game the conversation changed between Bennett and Clint, and they talked to the miner about his claim, and his day, and whatever else they could get him to talk about.

A half hour later a fourth miner came in and joined them, and then a fifth.

Two hours later not only did their table have six men at it, but so did the tables of the other men, Billy

London and Patch Brighton. Later still other games popped up at tables, and soon enough the din in the room was deafening.

As the liquor started to flow the women appeared, and with the women piano music. Clint hadn't noticed a piano before. Obviously it had been wheeled out from hiding.

The women began to work the men at the tables who weren't playing poker. In Clint's experience, women and poker didn't mix. Saloon girls seemed to know this, for they rarely tried to work a man while he was playing serious poker.

After a few hours of playing at a full table, Clint had come to two conclusions. One, miners were bad poker players, and two, Bennett was a good poker player. The former did not surprise him, but the latter did. Given the man's manner, he'd had his doubts about Bennett's abilities, but those doubts had been dispelled as he and the gambler proceeded to clean the miners out.

During the course of the game there had been a couple of fights in the saloon. Neither, however, had resulted in anyone being killed, so Clint assumed he still did not have a room for the night.

During a hand when he folded early, Clint had a chance to look around and study the women who were working the place. There were four, two blondes, a redhead, and a brunette. Whoever did the hiring apparently liked to stock a variety.

The blondes were very different. One looked to be in her twenties, very short and full-bodied, while the other was probably in her thirties, tall and willowy.

The brunette fell someplace between the two, more medium-sized.

The redhead, however, looked to be something special, and Clint wondered what she was doing in a mining town. She was tall—though not as tall as the willowy blonde—with masses of red hair falling down to her shoulders. Her skin was pale, and Clint wondered if she was freckled, because she was too far away to see that clearly. He assumed she would be. After all, she was a redhead. She had very long legs, and being special was more a matter of the way she moved than the way she looked. As she walked between the tables, most of the men—the ones whose heads were not down on the table—turned to watch her, even if they happened to be talking with one of the other girls at the time. Clint could see that the other women didn't like this, and he assumed that they didn't like the red-haired woman much. She didn't seem to care, though. In fact, she interacted very little with the other three women.

"You in?" one of the miners asked Clint.

Clint pulled his eyes and mind away from the girls and looked across the table at the miner, who was shuffling the cards.

"Go ahead and deal."

"I mean, if you wanna daydream that's okay with me," the man said. "That might be the only way we'll get some of our money back from ya."

"Don't worry," Clint said, with a smile, "my mind's on the game."

"Hey," the miner said, dealing, "*that's* what I'm worried about."

• • •

It was getting late enough so that Clint was wishing he had a room for the night when suddenly one of the men at Billy London's table started to shout.

"I know you been cheatin'," the man, a burly miner, said loudly.

The word "cheat" in a saloon attracted everyone's attention.

"Uh-oh," one of the miners at Clint's table said.

"What?" Clint asked.

"That's Lonnie Cord."

"So?"

"He's mean when he's drunk, and meaner when he thinks he's bein' cheated."

"How often does he think he's been cheated?" Clint asked.

"All the time," the miner said.

"That's because he loses all the time," one of the other miners at the table said.

"London can handle him," Bennett said.

"Maybe," the first miner said, "but Lonnie has a lot of friends."

"Are you fellas his friends?" Clint asked.

"Not us," the second man said, "but look at the bar."

Clint did so and saw three other miners watching the proceedings even more intensely than most of the men in the place.

"Are they armed?" Clint asked.

"Them and Cord."

At London's table he was speaking to the man, but his voice was so low they couldn't hear it.

"Never mind your smooth talk," Lonnie Cord shouted, not interested in what London had to say.

"Is London armed?" Clint asked Bennett.

"He's got a derringer."

If that was all the man was carrying, he was in trouble if Cord and his friends went for their guns. Clint slid his chair back from the table and dropped his hand down to his gun.

"I want my money back," Cord was shouting, "or I'm gonna start shootin'!"

Clint looked around, wondering if a lawman would bust in on the scene at any moment.

"Is there a sheriff in this town?" he asked Bennett.

"Yeah, and a good one, but he doesn't have any deputies. This could be all over by the time he gets here."

Clint decided that Billy London was going to have to handle Lonnie Cord all by himself. He was going to keep his eyes on the three miners at the bar.

"You gonna come up with my money, gambler?" Cord shouted.

London just stared at the man.

"Damn you—" Cord shouted and drew his gun.

Clint heard the report of the derringer, which he thought came from London's sleeve, but then he was looking at the men at the bar. All three of them drew their guns and Clint stood up shouting, "Don't!"

His shout distracted them for just a second, but that was long enough. By the time they decided to go ahead and fire at London, Clint was pulling the trigger on his own gun. There was no time for anything fancy so he just pumped a bullet into the thickest part of each man.

"Jesus—" he heard somebody say.

The three miners at the bar never got off a shot.

Clint walked to the three men to check them. They were dead. He straightened and was ejecting the spent shells from his gun, inserting live ones when Billy London approached him. The gambler was doing the same thing with his derringer.

"Looks like I owe you a drink," London said.

"At least," Clint said.

"Looks like you're out of luck, Clint," Vince said from behind the bar.

"Why's that, Vince?"

"None of these four fellas had a room here," the bartender said. "You still ain't got a place to sleep."

SIX

Clint and Billy London moved further down the bar so they could drink their beers without having to reach across the dead bodies.

"The sheriff should be here soon," Vince said, setting a beer in front of each of them.

"You'll enjoy meeting the sheriff," London said to Clint. "He's an interesting man."

Clint and London had exchanged names before moving further down the bar.

"If you say so," Clint said. He was annoyed because everyone in the saloon who had seen him draw would soon know who he was, especially once the sheriff arrived. After killing three men, it was going to be hard to keep it a secret.

"What brings you here, Adams?" London asked.

"Just passing through," Clint said.

"Is that what you're going to tell the sheriff?"

"What else should I tell him?"

"Hey, tell him whatever you want, it's just that you didn't look to me like a man who was just passing through today. You've, uh, been sitting in here quite a while."

"Are you going to tell him that?"

"Me? After what you just did? Hey, you lie and I'll swear to it." To illustrate his point he put his hand over his heart.

Billy London was something of a surprise to Clint. For one thing, up close the man was younger than he'd thought, and much younger than he would have expected. London appeared to be in his early forties, very well dressed in a black suit and a boiled white shirt. The other surprise was that he barely stood five foot five.

"Here he comes," London said, looking past Clint. "You're going to like this."

"Why—"

"The hand of the devil has been at work in here!" a voice boomed out over the room.

Clint turned and saw that the voice belonged to a tall, slender man wearing a badge and a preacher's collar. He turned and looked at London once, who smiled at him.

"You men, and you there, carry these men outside."

The men he pointed at exchanged glances, then shrugged and proceeded to do as they were told.

"Who killed these men?" the sheriff asked.

"I did," Clint said.

"And me," London spoke up.

The sheriff looked at them and then approached.

He was a couple of inches taller than Clint, and somewhere around thirty-five years old. Clint couldn't help but stare at the collar around his neck. Was this man a lawman, a man of the cloth . . . or both?

"We've already talked several times, Mr. London, since you first came to town."

"That's right, Sheriff."

"This is your first altercation. Was it unavoidable?"

"It was."

Now the sheriff looked at Clint.

"And your name?"

"Clint Adams."

The man recognized his name immediately.

"Well, well, and what brings such distinguished company to Chinaville?"

"I'm just passing through, Sheriff."

"And what was your part in this?"

"The three at the bar," Clint said. "They were mine."

"All three?"

"That's right."

"Why?"

"They were backing the one Mr. London killed."

The sheriff looked at London.

"A miner named Cord called me a cheater, Sheriff."

"And for that you killed him?"

"No," London said, "I didn't shoot him until he announced he was going to kill me and pulled his gun."

The sheriff looked at Clint.

"That's the way it was, Sheriff."

"And why did you kill these three men, Mr. Adams?"

"They were friends of the man Mr. London killed, and they took exception to it. They all drew."

"And what did you do?"

"I shouted a warning, which they ignored."

"And you killed them."

"Yes."

"I didn't hear that many shots," the sheriff said. "It must have been clean."

"It was," London said. "They never got off a shot."

"Why?" the sheriff asked.

"Why what?" London asked.

The sheriff didn't look at London at all, just kept staring at Clint, making it clear who he was talking to.

"Why what?"

"Why did you decide to help Mr. London?"

"He needed it," Clint said. "If I hadn't taken a hand he'd be dead now."

"I, for one, am glad that didn't happen," London said.

"Sheriff, the whole thing was clean," Vince said, from behind the bar. "Ask anybody."

The sheriff looked around the saloon once, and then back at Clint and London.

"Are we in trouble, Sheriff?" London asked.

"Not right now," the lawman—or cleric—said. "Mr. Adams, I hope you won't be killing anyone else while you're in Chinaville."

"I don't plan to," Clint said. "I didn't plan to kill these."

"Well," the sheriff said, looking around as the bodies were carried out, "you've killed three, let's make that your limit."

"Fine," Clint said, "it's a limit I can live with."

"Let's hope we all can, Mr. Adams." He started to walk away, then turned and said, "I'd like to see you in my office tomorrow morning, Mr. Adams."

"I'll try to make it."

"Don't try," the sheriff said, "do it. Let the Lord give your feet wings."

With that the sheriff with the clerical collar walked out.

SEVEN

"See?" Billy London said, turning to lean on the bar. "Isn't he interesting?"

"He didn't tell me his name." Clint also leaned on the bar, over his beer.

"Well, the locals call him 'Sheriff,' " London said, "or they call him 'Preacher.' There are even some who call him 'Preach.' "

"But what's his real name?"

London shrugged.

"Nobody seems to know."

"How did he get the job?"

London shrugged again.

"He had the job when I got here."

"And you never asked?"

"I wasn't that interested."

"But you said he was an interesting man."

London looked at Clint and said, "That doesn't mean I want to know his life's story."

Clint felt someone's presence at his elbow and turned to see Alex Bennett standing there holding something.

"Bennett."

"You comin' back to the table?" Bennett asked.

"Not tonight, I don't think so," Clint said. "Killing people puts me off my game."

"Here's your money, then," Bennett said, handing it to Clint. There was paper, coins, and some nuggets and bags of dust.

Clint noticed that Bennett and London never looked at each other.

"Yeah," London said, as Bennett sort of faded away, "killing puts me off my game, too. Did I hear right? You don't have a place to sleep?"

"That's right."

"There's another bed in my room," London said. "It's yours for as long as you like."

"That's real nice of you, Billy—"

"It's the least I can do for the man who saved my life," London said, "but there is one other thing."

"What's that?"

"Don't call me Billy."

"What should I call you?"

"London," the man said, "just London."

"All right, London," Clint said, "call me Clint."

"I'll tell Vince to give you a key to my room and have your stuff moved up there."

"I can get the key and take my gear up myself," Clint said. "If you don't mind, I think I'll go on up and turn in. I've had a long day."

"Sure, go ahead," London said. "Maybe we can

talk some more tomorrow, over breakfast."

"Sure, why not?" Clint said.

"Once again," London said, raising his beer glass, "thanks for your help."

Clint raised his glass as well. "My pleasure."

EIGHT

While Clint would have preferred to have had his own room, it was a relief to have a bed for the night. Before going up to the room he reminded Vince, the bartender and hotel desk clerk, that he still wanted his own room.

"First one that comes available is yours, Mr. Adams—guaranteed."

Satisfied that this was indeed the case, Clint went upstairs to sleep. He heard London come in during the night. He stayed awake without alerting the other man, waited until London himself had gotten into bed, and then went back to sleep.

In the morning he woke before London. There was a pitcher and basin in the room, but he decided he wanted a bath. He left the room without waking his temporary roommate and went downstairs to arrange for one.

The saloon was closed, but there was a man behind the hotel desk.

"Good morning, sir," he greeted Clint. "Can I help you?"

"I'd like a bath."

"Of course, sir," the clerk said. "I'll have one drawn for you. Warm, hot, or very hot?"

"Hot."

"Very well, sir." The clerk was in his forties, balding and watery-eyed, but polite.

"Is there someplace I can get some coffee while I'm waiting?"

"Just sit at a table, sir, and I'll have some coffee brought out. The bath shouldn't take too long to draw."

Clint moved into the empty saloon portion of the building and sat at a table. That's where he was when the front door opened and the sheriff entered.

"Good morning, Sheriff. I hope you're not looking for me."

"As a matter of fact, I was," the man said.

"I'm having coffee while I wait for a bath to be drawn," Clint said. "Why don't you join me?"

Clint thought the man might have quipped, "In the bath?" but this strange lawman with a collar didn't seem to have a sense of humor.

"I will, thanks."

"I didn't get your name last night."

"I didn't give it."

"So you're just 'the sheriff'?"

The man studied Clint for a few moments, then said, "My name is Virgil Train."

"Virgil—" Clint said, and then stopped short. It was a name he knew, and not one that he would have associated with either the law or the cloth. It was also a name he hadn't heard in a few years.

"I wondered what had happened to you."

"A lot of people probably wonder," Train said.

"You dropped out of sight for a while."

"And then showed up here."

"To become sheriff?"

"I came here to preach the word of God to the sinners who flock to mining towns like this one."

"And what happened?"

"They have no church, and they had no sheriff at the time."

"So you thought you'd combine both?"

"It seemed to be a challenge that God wanted me to take on," Train said, "so I took it."

Clint studied the man, and while he was doing it a woman came into the room carrying a tray with a pot of coffee and two cups.

"I saw you come in, Sheriff," she said, "thought you might like a cup."

"Thank you, Miss Jenny."

"Miss Jenny" was the full-bodied blonde Clint had been looking at the night before. Today she looked much better without the heavily made up face and the saloon girl dress, even better than the redhead he'd noticed. Her blond hair was worn in a braid that almost came to the middle of her back.

"Shall I pour for you?" she asked him.

"I think we can take care of that, thanks," he said.

"Sure," she said. The turn she executed was saucy,

and as she walked away she checked behind her to see if the two men were watching her. They were.

Clint leaned forward and poured two cups of coffee.

"What did you want to see me about . . . Sheriff?" he asked.

"I thought today you might want to tell me the real reason you're here," Train said, lifting his cup.

"What makes you think I didn't tell you that last night?"

"Call it a hunch."

"Well, your hunch is wrong, Sheriff," Clint said. "I'm just passing through, thought I might play some poker while I was at it."

"Thought you'd take some of that gold from the miners?" Train asked.

"It's a possibility."

"I've got professional gamblers like London and Bennett and others tryin' that, Mr. Adams. What makes you think you can—" He stopped short and asked instead, "You haven't become a professional gambler, have you? A professional poker player?"

"I like to think that I could if I wanted to," Clint said, "but no, that's not my intention." He saw no reason to fill the man in on his bet with Rick Hartman.

"Your reputation with a gun . . . are you trying to change that?"

Clint smiled at the lawman/preacher and asked, "You're not telling me you don't think that can be done, are you, Sheriff?"

NINE

"Is that your intention, then?" Train asked.

"No, Sheriff, it's not my intention," Clint said.

Train studied Clint, wordlessly working on his cup of coffee.

"Why is this so hard to believe, Sheriff?" Clint asked.

"I have found, Mr. Adams," Train said, "that men generally go to great lengths to live up to their reputations."

"You've found that, have you?"

"Yes, I have."

"As I recall," Clint said, "you have quite a reputation yourself, Mr. Train."

"That was Virgil Train," the sheriff said. "I am no longer that man."

"It's still your name."

"I am not the same Virgil Train, then."

"So you don't think that I could be another Clint

Adams? Maybe a different one from the one you've heard about?"

"I'm sorry," Train said, putting his cup down on the table, "no, I don't think so. I think that whatever your real reason is for comin' to Chinaville, you have not yet told me about it."

Train stood up.

"I'm sorry you feel that way, Sheriff," Clint said. "I would think that a man of the cloth—you are a man of the cloth, aren't you? I mean, that collar is for real, isn't it?"

Train touched the collar and said, "Yes, it is."

"And yet," Clint said, "if I arrived here with a collar on you wouldn't have believed it, would you?"

"No, I would not."

Clint poured himself another cup of coffee.

"Sheriff—Train—I think you have a lot of soul searching to do."

"How dare you—"

"Charity begins at home, isn't that the saying? A man of the cloth would give me the benefit of the doubt."

"A lawman would not."

"I'd be willing to bet," Clint said, looking Train in the eye, "that you've been a lawman even less time than you've been a preacher."

Train glared at Clint.

"I'm not trying to get on your bad side, Sheriff," Clint said, "I'm just trying to figure out how many sides you have. In fact, I wonder if you even know the answer to that."

"We will talk again, Mr. Adams," the sheriff said.

"I look forward to it, Sheriff."

Clint poured another cup of coffee as he watched the man walk out of the saloon.

Virgil Train left the saloon and crossed the street, heading for his office. It annoyed him that Clint Adams seemed to be able to look inside of him to see the conflict that raged there. Although Train was no longer the killer that everyone knew him to be in his old life, before he found God, there were still two Trains inside of him. First there was Sheriff Virgil Train. He'd held the job only six months, but already he felt as if he was born to it. And yet, Preacher Virgil Train was not yet ready to give up his quest, which was to spread the word of the Lord to as many people—as many sinners—as possible. That had been his quest for the past six years. When he arrived in Chinaville and took on the job as sheriff, it seemed to him to be the perfect marriage. People *had* to listen to Sheriff Train when they would not have necessarily listened to Preacher Train. By holding both jobs he was doing twofold work against sinners, instead of just one, and yet . . .

Clint Adams was right about one thing. There was a conflict. Where Sheriff Train was suspicious of people, Preacher Train should have been charitable. It was a conflict he'd been unable to resolve, but one that he'd been able to keep hidden.

Apparently, until now.

The girl, Jenny, came out and announced to Clint that his bath was ready.

"Thank you, uh, Miss Jenny."

"Just call me Jenny," she said. "It's only the Preacher who calls me 'Miss.' "

"Preacher? Is that how you think of him? Not as the sheriff?"

She shrugged.

"When he first came to town he was just the Preacher. He became the sheriff later. I call him Preacher. He doesn't seem to mind."

"Tell me," Clint said, "before he became the sheriff did he ever come over here to visit any of the girls?"

"Nope."

"And since?"

"Nope," she said, "not before or since." She stood with her hands behind her back, rocking left and right. "You gonna take that bath before it cools off?"

"Yep," he said, standing up.

"Want some company?"

"Uh, I'd love it," he said, "but I'd only be paying for the bath."

"That's okay," she said. "I'm feelin' pretty dirty. I could use a bath, too."

TEN

When Clint and Jenny entered the room where the tub was, steam was rising from the water.

"Good," she said, unbuttoning her dress, "it's still hot."

Clint watched as she unabashedly shed her dress and stood naked before him. Her breasts were pear-shaped and firm, her waist trim, sweeping out to wide hips, glorious buttocks, and long legs.

"You don't look dirty to me," he said.

"You, on the other hand," she said, "definitely need a bath. Get those clothes off and get into the tub. I'll wash you."

He matched her lack of shyness by shedding his clothes quickly and getting into the tub.

"Ouch," he said, easing himself in, "I told them hot, not very hot."

"Stop bein' a baby," she said, kneeling by the tub. She picked up the sponge and soap and began to lather his chest. Up from the water, like some miniature monster, his penis swelled.

"My," she said, "that looks real dirty."

She reached for it with two hands and began to soap it.

"Jesus—" he said.

She laughed, released him, and proceeded to climb into the tub with him. The tub was a big one, certainly big enough for the both of them, but with both of them in it some of the water spilled out onto the floor.

"My turn to soap you," he said, reaching for the soap. He worked up a lather between his hands, then began rubbing them over her breasts. Her wet skin gleamed and her nipples swelled. She lifted her legs and set them outside of him so she could scoot closer. They put their arms around each other and kissed, and he felt her rubbing her crotch up against his testicles and the base of his penis.

He slid his hands down her back until he was cupping her buttocks, then he lifted her up and brought her down again so that he could enter her. She gasped and then laughed, putting her arms around his neck. She started riding him up and down, and more water splashed from the tub onto the floor. He pulled her to him so he could kiss her wet neck and breasts and suck her nipples. She ran her nails over his back, causing him to shiver. Her movements became more frenzied and for just a moment he wished they had saved this for a bed, but then he stopped thinking and began moving with her until there was almost no water left in the tub. . . .

* * *

Later they got out of the tub and she said, "How would you like to try that in a bed?"

He smiled and said, "Lead the way."

They dried themselves off, dressed quickly, and he followed her to her room. . . .

ELEVEN

"I don't usually do this, you know," Jenny said later. They were in her room, getting dressed again after spending a couple of hours in her bed.

"Do what?"

"You know, have sex just for, well—"

"For free?"

"Yeah."

"Why this time?"

"Well . . . a girl gets an itch every once in a while," she said.

"And me?"

"You looked like you could scratch it."

"And did I?"

She widened her eyes and said, "Oh, yeah."

"Well, that's good," Clint said. "As long as I performed a service."

"Hey," she said, "you're not insulted, are you?"

"Well . . ."

46

"The way you're feelin' right now? It's the way a lot of us feel, you know, after?"

Clint thought about that a moment.

"It's not a good feeling, is it?" he asked.

"No, it surely ain't," she said. "I mean, we do perform a service, you know? But we still like to be treated like people."

"I can understand that."

She went to him and kissed him warmly.

"Thank you, Clint. You were wonderful."

He kissed her back and said, "So were you."

"Will you be stayin' in town awhile?" she asked. "You know, in case I get another itch?"

He smiled and said, "I'll be around."

"Good. I could use a beer right now. How about you?"

"Sounds good."

He strapped on his gun and then saw her watching him.

"You wear that all the time?"

"All the time," he said.

"You got some kind of rep?"

"Some kind," he said, and left it at that. They'd exchanged first names, but not last, and that suited him.

They left her room and started downstairs.

"Who owns this place, Jenny? Is it Vince?"

"Vince manages it," she said. "He works the bar, the desk, and he's the manager."

"That's a lot of work for one man. Who's the owner?"

"To tell you the truth, I don't know," she said.

"Vince hired me, he's the one who pays me, and he's the only one I see."

"Is it the same with the other girls?"

"I think so. Maybe a couple of them who have been here longer than me—Kate, Shelley—maybe they've seen the owner, but I don't think the rest of us have."

When they reached the first level, he saw that the saloon had opened for business while they were upstairs.

"Oh, one thing," she said.

"What?"

"Don't tell Vince what we did, okay? He won't like it that I gave it away."

Clint thought about the manner in which Vince had been treating him since he found out who he was and said, "I don't think he'll complain, but okay, I can keep quiet."

"You go up to the bar first and ask for a beer. I'll follow and get mine further down the bar. I'll see you later tonight when I'm working."

"Okay, Jenny."

He entered the saloon and went up to the bar, where Vince was cleaning glasses.

"Hey, Mr. Adams," Vince said. "I was looking for you before, in Mr. London's room."

"Did you wake him up?"

Looking sheepish, Vince said, "Yeah, I'm afraid I did, but how was I to know he was alone last night. He usually takes one of the girls with him."

"Can I get a beer?"

"Sure."

When Vince brought back the beer, Clint asked,

"What did you want with me?"

"I got you a room of your own. You can move in anytime."

"That's great. Thanks. What room?"

"Fourteen. Down the hall from Mr. London's room. Here's your key."

The bartender handed over the key and Clint took it and pocketed it.

"I'll wait for London to wake up before I go up to get my things," Clint said. "Meanwhile, after this beer I'll take a look around town."

"Ain't much to see," Vince said, " 'specially when it rains like it did last night."

"It rained last night?"

"Like hell. There's nothing out there but puddles and bigger puddles."

"Still," Clint said, "I'd like to take a look around town."

"Well, okay, suit yourself, but watch out you don't drown in one of them big puddles."

Clint finished his beer and set the empty mug on the bar.

"I'll be real careful, Vince."

"Hey, Vince," Jenny called, appearing at the end of the bar, "can I have a beer?"

Clint walked past her on the way to the front door and winked.

TWELVE

Two steps out the door and Clint's right foot was ankle-deep in a mud puddle. He pulled it up and the muck released it with a wet, squishy sound. As far as the eye could see Chinaville was mired in mud and puddles. Clint wondered how this would affect the people who lived or worked in tents. And what about the miners? Were they on high enough ground to avoid this? Or were they dealing with mountains that were becoming waterfalls?

Clint decided to be adventurous and try to get at least once around the town. There were not board-walks in front of every building, but somebody had tried to bridge the puddles with pieces of wood six to eight inches wide. In one place he even walked over an old door that someone had put down over a puddle.

Crossing the street was a real adventure. He finally came to a point where someone had laid several two-by-six pieces of wood end to end across the street, but when he got to the middle of the street passing wagons had buried those pieces, and he found himself up to his ankles again until he reached the next piece of wood.

By the time he reached the other side of the street his legs were tired from pulling his feet out of the muck. He found himself in front of a small saloon and decided to go inside.

It was still early, so the place was empty except for a sleepy-looking bartender and one man sitting at a corner table nursing a beer. The man was Sheriff Virgil Train—or, as some people called him, the Preacher.

"Can I get a beer?" Clint asked the bartender.

"Why not?" the man asked. "I'm runnin' a saloon here, ain't I? Ain't got but one customer, and I probably won't have that many more the rest of the day, so you sure can have a beer, mister, and thanks for comin' in to buy it."

As the man gave him the beer Clint asked, "Competition that tough that you can't get some customers?"

"It's him," the man said, jerking his thumb at Train. "As long as he's here nobody will come in."

"Why not?"

"They're afraid."

"Of him?"

"Of him, or of bein' too near him when somebody tries to kill him."

"Has that happened?"

"Lots of times."

"Anybody else ever been killed for being with him?"

"Not yet. Maybe you wanna test it out?"

Clint grinned and said, "I just might, at that. I guess the sheriff doesn't get to talk to too many people, huh?"

"Except on Sunday, when he preaches."

"People go to hear him preach, huh?"

"They're afraid not to."

"Aren't they afraid somebody will try to kill him while he's preaching?"

"It's more likely somebody would try to kill him while he's law-mannin'," the bartender said, "or while he's just settin' havin' a drink. It'll probably happen in my place, too. That's the kind of luck I got."

"Well," Clint said, picking up his beer, "I guess I'll just see if the sheriff wants some company."

"Sheriff," the bartender said, "Preacher, whatever, he'll probably just tell ya to go away."

"No harm in trying."

Clint took his beer and walked across the floor to where Train was sitting. He was sure that the man was aware of his presence, but he never looked up from the table he was sitting at. On the table was a half-filled mug of beer, and the sheriff's black hat. The man's hair was straight, unruly around his collar, black shot with gray.

"Mind if I have a seat?" Clint asked.

Now Train looked up at him.

"If you ain't afraid of gettin' shot at," Train said, "suit yourself."

Clint sat.

THIRTEEN

"Why do I get the impression you're not the most popular guy in Chinaville?" Clint asked.

"That's easy," Train said. "I uphold the law, *and* I preach to them. That's two reasons not to like me."

"I don't think anyone would try to shoot you for preaching," Clint said. "Sounds like you've been shot at by people who don't like lawmen."

"Naw," Train said, shaking his head while he played with his beer mug, turning it around and around. "You know what it's like to have a rep, Adams."

"But you're trying to live yours down."

"That's true, but there's always some hothead who comes to town and recognizes me and decides he's gonna notch his gun by shooting me from ambush. You must run into that."

"I have," Clint said, "but mostly I run into men who want to try me face-to-face. They figure that by planting me they'll make a big name for themselves."

Train looked at Clint with interest.

"You ever been beat to the draw?"

"You mean beat fair and square?"

"I mean," Train said, "beat, for whatever reason."

"Once."

Train looked surprised.

"What happened?"

"A kid ran across the street just as we were about to slap leather," Clint said. "A little girl. I didn't want to hit her, so I didn't fire."

Clint became aware that Train was staring at him with more intensity.

"Is this some kind of joke?" the lawman asked.

"I don't think so. If it is, it's on me, too. What are you talking about?"

"What happened to the little girl?"

"Nothing. She wasn't hurt."

"And you?"

"I took a bullet in the chest. It almost killed me."

"And the man who shot you?"

"I found him, later."

"Is he still alive?"

"No."

Train was still frowning.

"You want to tell me what's wrong with my story?"

"Nothin'," Train said, "except that it's my story, too."

"What do you mean?"

"Same situation," Train said. "A little girl ran between us, only I wasn't as good as you. I couldn't stop in time."

"You fired?"

He nodded.

"And hit the little girl?"

"Killed her."

"And what happened to you?"

"I took a bullet, and nearly died."

"And the man who shot you?"

"I haven't seen him."

"And killing the little girl, is that what drove you to the cloth?"

"Yes."

"But you couldn't put your gun down?"

"No," Train said, "for two reasons."

"One of which we've already talked about. If you put it down, one of those back-shooters would have killed you by now."

"That's right."

"And second?"

"Nobody would listen to me when I preached," Train said, "not without the gun on my hip. I wear the gun, everybody listens."

"And you think you're accomplishing what you want?"

"I'm gettin' the word of God out," Train said. "That's what I want."

"How did you manage to get elected sheriff when nobody likes you?" Clint asked.

"I wasn't elected," he said. "I was appointed. When I came here there was no law, and it wasn't safe to stick your head out a window, let alone walk the streets."

"Why no sheriff?"

"Of the last four they had," Virgil Train explained, "three of them were shot dead and the fourth was run out of town."

"So they offered you the job?"

Train shook his head.

"It wasn't offered. I asked for it."

"And got it."

"Yes."

"And did they try to run you out of town?"

"They did."

"Needless to say," Clint concluded, "they didn't succeed."

"No, they did not. I'll leave Chinaville when I feel my mission here is done."

So, Clint thought, he's a man on a mission. But which mission? he wondered. To bring law and order to Chinaville . . . or to bring God?

FOURTEEN

"What are you doin' here, anyway?" Train asked.

"I was just taking a look at the town," Clint said.

"Not much to see on a day like this," Train said. "Most of it's covered in mud."

"I see that now," Clint said.

Train sat back and looked at Clint with interest for the first time. Clint thought that the man's mood had suddenly changed, and he wondered if that happened a lot. A man with mood swings did not often make a good lawman.

"You seem in the mood to talk today," Train said.

Clint shrugged.

"Just passing the time."

"You want to pass it by tellin' me the real reason you're in Chinaville?"

"If I tell you the real reason, are you going to believe me?" Clint asked.

"Try me."

Clint thought a moment, then decided, why not? He went ahead and told Train the story of his bet with Rick Hartman to see how much money he could make gambling.

Train studied Clint all the while he was listening to him, and then continued for a few moments after.

"I believe you," he finally said.

"Why?"

"That's too crazy a story not to be true. You rode all the way here just to win a bet?"

"Well, not just to win a bet—well, yeah, that's mostly the reason—what's wrong with that?"

"I don't know," Train said. "I've never been a gambling man. I never played cards or roulette. I don't remember ever making a bet with anyone."

"About anything?" Clint asked, surprised.

Train shook his head.

"Not that I can recall."

"Have you always been this serious a man?"

"I've always been kind of serious, yes," Train said, "but—"

"But what?"

Train didn't answer.

"Even more since the death of the little girl?"

"The death I caused," Train said. "I killed her."

"You didn't deliberately kill her, Train, it was an accident. There's a difference."

"I know there is."

"Then why are you so hard on yourself?"

Train leaned forward, resting his forearms on the table on either side of his beer mug.

"You've been truthful with me, so I will be truthful with you."

He stopped, and Clint didn't push him. He just waited.

"I see her every day," Train said finally. "Every time I close my eyes, I see her. But you know what's funny?"

"What?"

"I don't see her dead. I see her alive. I see her in my dreams, alive and smiling. That's why I hardly sleep anymore."

"I don't understand."

Train looked at him.

"What don't you understand?"

"You've discovered God, isn't that right? As a result of this . . . accident?"

"That's right."

"Then why isn't He giving you more comfort?"

"Maybe I don't deserve comfort," Train said immediately. "Maybe I was supposed to discover God and pass along His word—"

"And suffer along the way?"

"Exactly."

Clint looked dubious, taking a swig of his beer to try to cover his doubt.

"Tell me something, Adams."

"I will if you call me Clint."

"Very well, Clint . . . do you believe in God?"

Clint frowned. He should have expected this question to pop up once he got into a conversation with a preacher. The problem was he didn't think of Train as a preacher, but as a sheriff.

"If there is a God," he said, "I don't think you have to suffer to believe in Him."

"I serve Him—"

"Or to serve Him," Clint said. "It seems to me that most religions believe that you have to suffer in order to serve God."

"And you don't believe this?"

"To tell you the truth, Sheriff—"

"Virgil."

"—Virgil, to tell you the truth I don't know what I believe. I've seen too many awful things that I don't think a great and powerful supreme being should have allowed to happen."

"God has His reasons."

"And man won't ever know them," Clint said. "That doesn't strike me as fair."

"When we all meet on Judgment Day, then we will know," Train said.

Clint finished his beer and stood up.

"Virgil, I for one don't relish waiting that long."

"Clint, suddenly I'm glad you came to Chinaville."

"Why?" Clint asked suspiciously.

"Because I think I can save you."

Suddenly, Clint wasn't so glad he had come to Chinaville.

FIFTEEN

Clint finished his tour of Chinaville, which looked as if it had sunk a few feet that day. Before entering the Buckhorn Saloon, he kicked off as much mud as he could.

Inside he saw that the place did not have much more life than when he'd left. It looked just about the way it had when he first arrived yesterday. The three gamblers were once again at their tables, playing solitaire and nursing drinks, waiting for the miners to appear.

Vince was behind the bar and noticed him as soon as he entered. Even before he got to the bar, there was a beer waiting for him there.

"Thanks, Vince."

Clint took the beer and walked to Billy London's table. In order to get there he had to walk past Bennett, to whom he nodded, and then Patch Brighton, who didn't look up.

"I see you're awake."

London looked up at him and smiled.

"I rarely get up before noon, Clint. To me, six A.M. is my time to go to bed, not to get up."

"Mind if I sit?"

"No, no, go ahead. I've already shared my room with you, why would I stop at sharing my table?"

Clint sat down. London had a fresh beer at his elbow, or he would have bought the man one.

"How did you do at Bennett's table last night?" London asked.

"Well," Clint said, "until you interrupted me I was doing okay."

"Why not try my table tonight?"

Clint laughed.

"I know your reputation, London. Why would I want to play poker with you?"

London smiled and leaned forward.

"Because I know your reputation, too, Clint. I know you've played in some big games with the likes of Luke Short and Bat Masterson. Why would you not want to play me?"

Under normal circumstances Clint would have loved to play Billy London, just to watch the man play, but because of his bet with Rick it didn't make sense for him to bump heads with a gambler of London's caliber.

"Maybe you'll see me sitting across from you one night," Clint said.

London sat back.

"What's holding you back?" he asked. "I know you're not afraid of me."

"It's a long story," Clint said. He'd already told one person about his bet with Rick today, he didn't feel like telling another.

"I'll take your word for it, Clint," London said. "After all, you did save my life."

"What do you think of Bennett, London?" Clint asked.

"Competent."

"And what about Patch Brighton?"

"Patch is good."

"How good?"

London smiled.

"Not as good as me," he said, "not as good as you. You know, you don't have to play at one of our tables. You could start your own."

"How would the others feel about that?"

"Bennett knows who you are, so he won't complain. I don't know about Patch."

"What kind of deal do you all have with the owner?" Clint asked.

"He gets a cut."

"Have you met him?"

"I haven't," London said. "I made my deal with Vince, there."

Clint turned and looked over at the bartender.

"Do you know anyone who has seen the owner?" he asked.

"No."

"What do you think?"

"About what?"

"About the possibility that Vince is the owner himself."

London shrugged.

"It wouldn't make much difference to me if he was," he said. "My deal would be the same."

"You've got a point."

"How about some two-handed?" London asked.

"I don't think so," Clint said. "I'm going to go upstairs and clean off my boots, and then maybe take a nap."

"Did you do somethin', uh, strenuous today?"

"Yes, I did," Clint said. "I tried to walk around this town in all the mud."

"If you're here long enough you'll learn not to go outside after it's rained."

"I've learned that already," Clint said, standing up. "By the way, I got my own room so I'll be taking my gear out of yours. Thanks again for taking me in."

"How would it look if I let the man who saved my life sleep in a barn? You're very welcome."

"I'll see you later tonight."

"Yes," London said, "you certainly will. Have a good rest, my friend."

Clint walked away from London's table, wanting very much to play against the man. If not for the bet, he would have. He wondered why he and Rick took these bets of theirs so damned seriously.

SIXTEEN

Clint collected his things from London's room and moved them to his own, room fourteen. Once inside he set about cleaning the mud off his boots, using some water, and then put them in the corner to dry. That done he stretched out on the bed to take a nap. His strenuous morning with Jenny and then his walk around town had tired him out. He wasn't going to be any good at a poker table if he couldn't see the cards.

It took only moments for him to fall asleep.

After Clint Adams left him, Virgil Train—Sheriff to some, Preacher to others, both to almost only himself—left the saloon and went back to his office.

There, seated behind his desk, he decided that one of the reasons God had sent him to Chinaville was to meet Clint Adams, the famous Gunsmith, and convince him that God really existed.

As big a reputation as Virgil Train had once had as a gunman, he knew it could not match that of the Gunsmith, whose legend was on a par with that of Wild Bill Hickok himself. As a man who had killed many men, Clint Adams was badly in need of saving—even if he had only killed a fraction of the men he was credited with.

During the months he had been serving as sheriff, Virgil Train had wondered what higher purpose he had been put here for. Was this it? To convince this one man to give up his gun and believe in the Lord? Once he believed that his purpose was to save the whole town, but how could one man do that when he didn't even have a church to preach in? And as sheriff he had become more like the man he once was than the man he wanted to be. Too many of the townspeople and miners steered clear of him because he was the law. Others because he was a preacher.

It seemed to him that neither of his chosen professions was very successful.

He looked up at the heavens and asked, "Have you brought me here only to fail? Or is my salvation the presence of Clint Adams?"

Of course, there was no answer.

Train thought about the bottle of whiskey in his desk. Sometimes, when he drank, he thought he heard God talking to him. Then, in the morning, he felt terrible, not physically from the drinking, but spiritually. When he drank, his thoughts became not those of the man he was, or the man he wanted to be, but the man he used to be. The old Virgil Train.

And the old Virgil Train was somebody he never wanted to be again.

Not if he could help it.

SEVENTEEN

When Clint awoke it was dark out. He'd slept longer than he'd intended, but he knew that by now things would be in full swing downstairs. He used the water in the pitcher and basin on the top of the dresser to wash up, then strapped on his gun and went downstairs.

The one edge he thought he might have had—his anonymity—had gone out the window with the shooting last night. By now everyone in town knew who he was. That was not enough, though, to make him give up on his bet. Now he would just have to depend on his poker-playing abilities.

When he got downstairs he saw that Bennett's table was full, as was Patch's. The only table with a chair empty was London's, and he doubted that was by accident.

He went to the bar first for a drink. Actually, he

was pretty hungry, but he didn't want to go outside in the mud again.

"You look well rested," Vince said, setting a beer down in front of him.

"I am, and hungry. Can I get a sandwich from you?"

"I got some chicken I can cut up and put on some bread."

"That'll do."

"Got some hard-boiled eggs, too."

"Okay," Clint said, "but no salt."

Saloons that put out hard-boiled eggs usually salted them heavily. It made men thirsty, and they drank more whiskey and beer.

Vince brought the eggs first, and Clint ate those while he waited for his sandwich. He turned to face the saloon with an egg in one hand and his beer on the bar. He didn't want anyone seeing him with both hands occupied. It might give them ideas.

Across the floor he saw Jenny walking around. She saw him and stood for a moment with her hands on her hips, smiling at him. As she walked to a table she swung her hips, and he knew it was for his benefit.

He studied the poker games going on at the tables of the three gamblers. There were a few other games going on, as well, and he looked them over. He didn't believe in coincidence, but London's table continued to be the only one with a chair available. How could the man have arranged that?

"Looks like if you want to play," Vince said, setting down a plate with three sandwiches on it, "you're gonna have to play Mr. London."

"Looks like it," Clint said, picking up one of the sandwiches.

"Think you can beat him?" Vince asked.

"I don't know."

"Nobody has," Vince said. "He makes money every night."

"Don't Bennett and Patch make money every night?" Clint asked.

"Well . . . yeah, I guess."

That was no surprise. They were professionals playing against a bunch of miners. They were supposed to win.

"But London's the best of the three," Vince said. "Ain't he?"

"Yes, Vince," Clint said, "I think he is."

One thing Clint could never resist when it came to poker was playing against someone who was supposed to be better than he was.

He finished a second sandwich, downed the beer, and paid Vince for both.

"You gonna play against him?" Vince asked excitedly.

"Yes, Vince, I am."

"This I gotta see."

Clint started away, then turned and pointed a finger at the bartender.

"If you're going to watch, watch from here, and don't—I repeat, *don't*—spread the word. I don't want a crowd around the table."

"Okay."

"Do you understand what I'm telling you?"

"Sure."

"Vince?"

"I understand, Mr. Adams," Vince said. "I won't say a word to nobody."

Clint nodded, hoping that Vince did indeed understand and would keep his word.

EIGHTEEN

"Well, well," Billy London said, looking up at Clint without betraying any hint of recognition, "a new player."

"Is this the fella you been savin' the chair for?" one of the miners asked.

London looked at the man and said, "I wasn't aware that I had been saving this chair for anyone, Mr. Sykes."

Sykes looked at London, then looked away, muttering, "Scarin' fellas away, I call that savin' the chair."

"Sit down, sir," London said. "We're playin' five-card stud. The minimum bet is one dollar, with no limit."

Clint was surprised, but then why should he have been? Weren't miners, men who were risking all, by nature gamblers? Some of them had given up homes and families to come up here and try to get rich. Why should they play poker any differently?

Clint pulled the empty chair out and sat down. It was London's deal, and he proceeded to deal each man one card down and one card up. London dropped a king of hearts in front of himself, but he gave Sykes an ace of spades. Clint had a jack of diamonds in front of him. When he checked his hole card he saw that it was a jack of clubs.

"Ace bets," London said.

"A dollar," Sykes said, still looking sour.

The man sitting between Clint and Sykes called, as did Clint. London called and the fifth man at the table, sporting a deuce, folded.

"Comin' out," London said, dealing out the third card.

Sykes got a ten to go with his ace, while London bought a second king. Clint received another jack, giving him a pair on the table and a third one in the hole. Three of a kind, an excellent hand in any form of poker game, but especially good in five-card stud.

"Five dollars," London said.

"I raise five," Sykes said, trying to make them think he had a pair of aces—only he hadn't bet strongly enough when he first got the ace. It was more likely he had a pair of tens, or nothing.

The other miner in the game folded. Clint called, wanting to see what London would do.

"I raise," he said. "Your five, and ten more."

Sykes stared at London's cards. Clint didn't know what the man was staring at. It was no secret he had kings, but did he have three?

"I call," Sykes said.

"Call," Clint said.

"Three players left," London said. "Cards comin' out."

Sykes got a queen, giving him a ten, ace, and queen on the table. If he had a king or jack in the hole he needed a card for a straight. With three jacks in front of him, and two kings in front of London, Clint didn't figure the miner to make his straight, but that didn't stop Sykes from betting. London had gotten a deuce.

London had the lead and bet ten dollars, even though Sykes had raised him earlier.

"I raise," Sykes said, even though London had already raised him.

Sykes was looking past Clint to London, so he was surprised when Clint said, "Raise, twenty."

Both Sykes and London looked at him, and at his cards. His jacks had been joined by a lowly four, no help. Why hadn't he raised earlier? He knew what they were thinking—or hoped they were thinking, anyway—that he now had jacks and fours. The last thing he wanted them to think was that he had three jacks.

"What the hell—" Sykes said, which was what Clint was thinking about the way the man was playing his hand.

"Interesting," London said. "I think I'll just call both raises—for now."

"Your two pair won't beat my straight, friend," Sykes said. He was sweating, and was obviously trying to talk Clint out of the hand.

"You've got to make your straight first, friend," Clint said.

Sykes looked down at his cards. Perhaps, if they'd been playing seven-card stud with one card to go, he could bluff, but not in this game. He still had to collect his fifth card.

"I'll call," Sykes said sourly.

"Last card," London said, and dealt them out.

Sykes got another ten, and suddenly—judging from the look on his face—Clint felt sure the man had three of them. He himself got a king, which didn't help him, but it certainly hurt London—who had bought another deuce. He had kings and deuces on the table. With a king in front of him and a deuce having been folded on the table, Clint felt reasonably sure that London did not have a full house. Still, odder things had happened in a poker game.

London, who had the lead with two pair, said, "I bet fifty."

It was too big a bet for the situation, and Clint felt sure he was trying to steal the hand.

"I raise," Sykes said quickly, treasuring his three tens. "Fifty more." He carefully measured out some gold nuggets, which he had obviously gotten weighed already. He knew exactly how many to bet to make up the fifty dollars.

The bet was a hundred to Clint. The only thing he knew for sure was that he had three jacks, and all he could do was bet them. He could try to figure out what the other two had all night, but he preferred to just play his cards in this instance.

"I call the hundred," he said, "and raise a hundred."

The game had quickly escalated from the one-dollar minimum.

Chuckling, London said, "I fold, Clint."

"Well, I don't fold," Sykes said. "I beat his two pair, and so do you, London."

"If I thought I beat his two pair I'd stay in, Sykes. I believe him. It's you I don't believe."

Whether he was trying to or not, London incited the man to raise even more than he'd intended.

"I'm raisin' my poke," Sykes said, tossing in a heavy bag of gold dust. It hit the table with an audible thump. "Two hundred."

As the dealer, London was still in charge of the table.

"It's a hundred-dollar raise to you, Clint. Sykes is all in."

Clint knew that if he raised again Sykes would have to borrow to call the bet or fold.

"I'll just call," he said.

"Hah!" Sykes said, turning his hole card over to reveal another ten. "Three tens. Beat 'em!"

He started to reach for the pot when London said, "He does beat them, Sykes. He's got three jacks. He's had them from the start."

"Wha—" Sykes said. He looked at Clint and said, "Show me."

Clint obliged him by turning over his third jack.

"Son of a—"

"Three jacks wins," London said.

Clint reached and drew in his pot, including the bag of dust.

"Wait a minute," Sykes said, "wait a minute. How did you know what he had? And what did you call him? Clint?"

"That's his name."

"You said you didn't know his name."

"I never said that, Sykes."

"And you were saving the chair for him."

"I wasn't."

"He's in it with you," Sykes went on. "That's the only way you could know what he had, if you bottom dealt him the three jacks."

"What?" London asked.

"You heard me."

"Sykes," London said, "everybody at the table knew what he had except you."

Sykes looked around and the other two miners nodded. It was why they had folded.

"Naw," Sykes said. "I don't believe it. How come I didn't know?"

"Because you're a piss-poor poker player, Sykes," London said. "Why don't you get out of that seat so somebody else can have it?"

Sykes looked around the table for help, but there was none to be had.

"I still think—"

London slammed his hand down on the table.

"If you call me a cheater one more time, Sykes, they're gonna be carryin' you out of here!"

Sykes glared at London for a few moments, but ultimately he wilted and looked away. He slid his chair back slowly, stood up, then turned and stormed to the door. Before he went out, though, he had a last say.

"I know you two cheated me!" he shouted, so everyone could hear him. "I'll get my money and gold back if it's the last thing I do!"

He turned then and went out the door quickly.

"You fellas better be careful," one of the other miners said. "Sykes is a hothead."

"We'll keep our eyes open," London said.

"I'm serious," the miner said. "He'll back-shoot either one of you."

"Thanks for the warning," Clint said.

"It was a well played hand, Clint," London said as the miner to his left gathered the cards for his deal. "Much too well played for the likes of him."

"Thank you, London."

London looked at the miner with the cards and said, "Deal, my friend."

NINETEEN

Clint played for a few hours and realized that he and London were taking in all the money. A new player sat down in Sykes's chair and lasted only about an hour before he tapped out. Later, one of the other miners left, leaving the table with two empty chairs.

Caught between Clint and London, the last miner finally tossed in his cards and said, "I'm through. You guys are too lucky tonight."

He got up and left.

London shuffled the deck and looked across the table at Clint.

"You think he's right?"

"About what?"

"That we're too lucky tonight?"

Clint smiled.

"I just think we're too good for them."

"You got that right." The gambler stopped shuffling. "You want to play two-handed?"

"You know what happens if we do that long enough, don't you?"

"Sure," London said, "we break even—but it's something to do. And maybe while we're at it someone else will sit down."

"Okay," Clint said, "then deal."

Rather than having anyone sit down with them, Clint and London ended up playing to a crowd. First there was a curiosity about two men playing poker against each other, and then the game itself—between two good poker players—got interesting.

In two-handed poker evenly matched players will almost invariably end up back where they started from if they play long enough. There's no bluffing with only two players, so it's virtually always the man with the better cards who wins. It's better to set a time limit in two-handed poker because the time will run out while one man is hot and getting all the cards, leaving the other with no time to get hot himself, and then get even. Clint and London, however, did not set a time limit and since no one would sit down with them they played until they were the last two men in the saloon. Even Bennett and Patch, the other two professional gamblers, had gone to their rooms when their tables emptied out. Finally, there were only three men left in the place, Clint, London, and Vince, the bartender.

"If you fellas don't quit now," Vince said, "I'll leave you the keys to lock up."

"Just this last hand," London said. "If I win it, I'll be ahead."

Sure enough he took the hand, and when they tallied up their pokes, London had won five dollars from Clint.

"Call it even," Clint said.

"Oh no," London said, "I've got a five-dollar edge and I'm going to count it."

For the night, however, both men were up considerably more than five dollars. Clint thought he could probably go back to Labyrinth now and win his bet if he and Rick hadn't set a time limit. He still couldn't go back to Labyrinth for at least two weeks.

"Can I go to bed now?" Vince asked as both men stood up.

"One last drink, Vince," London said, "and then off you go."

"What'll it be?"

"Beer?" London asked Clint.

"Beer," Clint said.

"Beer," London said to Vince.

"Beer," Vince said. "I heard you the first time."

He drew the two men their beers, locked the front door, and said, "Put out the lights when you go to bed."

"See you in the mornin', Vince," London said.

Vince just waved and went to his room.

London took a sip of his beer, leaned on the bar, and regarded Clint.

"You're a good poker player."

"Thanks."

"You've the instincts to do this for a living."

"You think so?"

"Oh yeah," London said, "you just need to do it

and do it and do it to get it right."

"You think I'm as good as you?"

London laughed.

"Oh no," he said, "you're not going to get me with that."

"With what?"

"If I say no, you're not as good as me, you'll be after me the rest of the time you're here, dogging me, wanting to play me all the time."

"Huh."

"And if I say yes, you are as good as me—well, that would be a lie."

Clint stared at the man for a few moments, then laughed, soon to be joined by London.

"You're a son of a bitch, London, you know that?"

"I'm afraid I've been told that many times, my friend," London said, "and I'm sure that I shall hear it many more times, as well."

TWENTY

When Clint got to his room he knew someone was inside. He also knew who it was. It was instinct, basically, but it was also the scent of perfume.

"Are you in my bed, Jenny?" he asked, entering the room.

"Do you mind?"

"No," he said. He reached up and turned the flame higher on the lamp. The room became bathed in yellow light. She was lying under the sheet, but it was molded to her and he knew she was naked beneath it. The outline of her big breasts and long waist excited him. He put his winnings on the dresser. He hefted Sykes's bag of gold before setting it down.

"How did you do?" she asked while he undressed.

"I did all right."

"I know you beat the miners out of some money," she said. "I meant how did you do against London?"

He sat on the bed and took off his boots.

"He won five dollars from me."

She sat up, and the sheet fell away, revealing her breasts. He turned to look at her. In the light from the lamp her skin looked golden.

"You were playin' all this time?"

"Yep."

"And you broke even?"

"Nope," Clint said. "He won't call it even. He's up five dollars."

"Competitive little fella, isn't he?"

"He's a gambler."

"And you're not?"

"Not by profession."

"What are you by profession?"

He thought a moment, then said, "A layabout."

"I don't think so."

"I'm independently wealthy?"

"I don't think you'd be here takin' money from the miners if you were."

He shrugged.

"Then I don't have a profession."

"Did you ever?"

"Once I was a lawman," Clint said, "but that was a long time ago."

"Want to talk about it?"

"Do you want to talk about what brought you here?" he asked.

"No."

"Then I don't want to talk, either," he said.

"Okay," she said, opening her arms to him, "then let's not talk."

He discarded the remainder of his clothes and joined her on the bed.

"Turn down the lamp," she said.

"No."

"Why not?"

He kissed her right nipple and she shivered.

"Because in the lamplight you look like you're made from gold."

She caught her breath.

"My, my," she said, after a moment, "you certainly know what to say to a girl, don't you?"

He kissed her neck and she smelled of perfume and a bath. She smelled so clean and fresh that it excited him. He kissed both breasts, then her belly, her navel, her pelvis, and finally worked his tongue through the fine blond hair between her legs. She smelled fresh there, too, but when he touched her with his tongue she became wet and gave off another, even more exciting odor.

"Oh, God . . ." she said as his tongue played over her, gently at first, and then more insistently. Suddenly she was overtaken by such waves of pleasure that she put her hands on his head and tried to push him away.

"You're . . . killin' . . . me," she said haltingly, pounding on his shoulders.

He took his mouth away, then raised himself over her and plunged into her. She gasped and instead of pushing him away this time wrapped her arms and legs around him so he *couldn't* get away.

TWENTY-ONE

Virgil Train was in his office early the next morning when a man came bursting in.

"You better come quick, Preacher—uh, I mean, Sheriff."

"What is it?" The man looked familiar, but try as he might Train could not come up with his name.

"A dead man," the man said. "He's been shot . . . in the back!"

Train stood up.

"Show me."

He followed the man outside. Although it hadn't rained the night before, the streets were still muddy. The number of deep puddles had decreased at least. Now there were just bogs, like quicksand.

Train followed the man over to the alley next to the saloon and hotel. There was a crowd waiting there for them. Train went into the alley and saw a man lying facedown in the mud. There was a single bullet wound in the center of his back.

"Anybody know who he is?" Train asked.

"We ain't turned him over, Preacher," someone said.

"Sheriff, you jerk," another voice said. "He's the sheriff now."

"Well, he's a preacher, too," the other man argued. "He could say a few words over him."

"More likely he's got to find out who killed him."

Train looked at the man who had led him there and suddenly the name came to him.

"Jakes, turn him over for me."

"Sure, Preach—I mean, Sheriff."

Jakes leaned over and turned the dead man onto his back. The face was hidden by mud.

"Clean his face."

"I ain't got nothing—" Jakes started, but Train took out a white handkerchief and handed it to him. Using it, he started trying to clean the face, but it was slow going.

"Look out," somebody shouted, and suddenly a bucket of water was dumped onto the dead man.

"Who did that?" Train shouted. "It's disrespectful of the dead!"

"Maybe so," somebody said, "but it worked. Look."

Train looked down at the dead man and had to admit, it *had* worked. The water had cleaned all of the mud from the man's face.

"Okay, anyone know him?" Train asked.

"That's Sykes," someone said.

"He a miner?" Train asked.

"Yeah," a man said, "he's got a Cripple Creek claim, him and his brothers."

"They ain't gonna like this," a voice said.

"Well, I don't like it, either," Train said. "Somebody go and get the undertaker."

"I know who killed him," a man said.

Train found the man who belonged to the voice.

"You stay here," he told him. "Everybody else move out. Jakes, you stay. You'll help the undertaker carry the body away."

"Yes, sir."

"Okay, the show's over," Train shouted at the men. "Get!"

Slowly the men wandered away and Train moved closer to the man who'd said he knew who killed Sykes.

"You saw who did this?" Train asked.

"Well, no—"

"Then how can you say you know who did it?"

"He was in the saloon last night, and he had an argument."

"With you?"

"Two fellers," the man said. "That gambler, London, and that new feller in town, the one killed three men the first night he was here."

"Adams."

"Huh?"

"Clint Adams?"

Obviously, the man hadn't known who Adams was, but now he did.

"That was the Gunsmith?"

Train ignored the question.

"What was the argument about?"

"Sykes said they cheated him out of his gold."

"How bad did he lose?"

"He tapped out."

"Any guns drawn?"

"No. London told him to get out before he killed him."

"He said that?"

"Well . . . somethin' like that."

"And what did Sykes say?"

"He said he was gonna get his poke back if it was the last thing he done."

Train took a moment to think. He didn't remember Sykes, so he knew nothing about him and his brothers.

"How well do you know this man?" he asked Jakes and the other man.

"His first name's Harley," Jakes said, "and he's got three brothers. They're mean, Sheriff."

"Why don't I know them?"

"They don't come into town much," the other man said. "Only Harley did that, to play poker."

Train looked away and saw the undertaker slogging through the mud toward them.

"All right, you two help the undertaker get the body over to his office. Jakes, you know how to get to the Sykes claim?"

"Yes, sir."

"I'll meet you at the undertaker's with two horses."

"W-what for?"

"You're going to take me to their claim."

"For what?"

"So I can tell them their brother is dead."

"Do I gotta?" Jakes asked. "They're a mean bunch, Sheriff."

"Yes, Jakes," Train said patiently, "you gotta."

TWENTY-TWO

The knock on the door woke Clint, who slid his arm from beneath Jenny's head without waking her to answer it.

"Sorry to bother you so early, Clint," Virgil Train said. The man looked past Clint at the woman in his bed and gave him a disapproving look.

"Are you here as a sheriff or as a man of the cloth?" Clint asked.

"As sheriff," Train said. "A man was found dead this morning in the alley next to this building."

"And?"

"He was shot in the back."

"Why are you telling me this?"

"His name was Harley Sykes."

"Sykes," Clint said. "I played poker with a man named Sykes last night."

"The same one. I heard there was some trouble."

"Not much."

"An argument?"

"Not much of one," Clint repeated.

"I heard Sykes threatened you and London."

"He shouted something on his way out," Clint said, "but I didn't catch it."

"Listen to me," Train said. "Sykes has some brothers and I've been told they're a bad bunch. I'm going out to tell them about their brother this morning."

"And you're going to tell them about the argument? That their brother thought he was cheated at poker?"

"Was he?"

"He was just a bad poker player, Sheriff." Clint was angry but didn't want to show it.

"I'm gonna want to talk to you and London when I get back," Train said.

"Talk to some of the other people who were in the saloon, too, Sheriff," Clint said. "Talk to Vince."

"I'm gonna talk to everyone, Clint," Train said. "I want to find out who killed this man. No matter what he did, he didn't deserve to die facedown in the mud with a bullet in his back."

"I'll tell London when I see him. I'll be available for you when you get back."

"And London?"

Clint shrugged.

"I can't speak for him."

"Fair enough. Just tell him I'll be wanting to talk to him."

"I'll tell him," Clint said, "if I see him."

Train looked like he was going to say something else, but instead said, "Fine," and left.

Clint closed the door and went back to the bed, where Jenny was waiting with her eyes open and the sheet pulled up to her neck.

"What did he want?"

"Sykes, one of the men I played poker with last night," Clint said, "was shot in the back last night."

"And he thinks you did it?"

"I don't believe so," Clint said, "but he knows that Sykes thought he was cheated last night by me and London."

"That's ridiculous," Jenny said. "That man was a bad poker player and everyone knew it. His *brothers* knew it, that's why they tried to keep him from coming to town all the time."

"You know them?"

She looked away and said, "Lots of the girls know them. They used to come to town together all the time, but they were always getting into trouble, so they stopped—except for Harley. He's the youngest and he just kept comin' to town, mostly to play poker."

"Aren't his brothers mad that he's losing their gold?" Clint asked.

"Of course, but he's been losing his share of the gold, not theirs. They've seen to that."

"What is their reaction going to be to his death?"

Her eyes widened and she said, "They're gonna go crazy. I mean, they fight among themselves a lot, but Harley was their baby brother. They're gonna go nuts."

He sat in silence for a few moments, then said, "I've got to talk to London."

"Clint," she said, "come back to bed with me where it's warm."

He would have much preferred to do that, but he couldn't. He had to warn London, not only about Train, but about the Sykes brothers, as well.

He leaned over, kissed her, and said, "I can't, Jenny. I'd really like to, but—"

"It's okay," she said. "You go and warn London. I'll be here."

"I'll see you later."

He dressed quickly, left the room, and hurried down the hall to London's room.

TWENTY-THREE

London continued to look bleary-eyed at Clint while Clint explained first about Train's visit and then what Jenny had told him.

"I know a lot of this already," London said, rubbing his eyes. "Sykes's brothers came in plenty of times to drag him away from one poker table or another. Finally they stopped comin' and he kept comin'."

"Did you ever have words with them?"

"No. Does Train think I killed him?"

"I don't know what Train thinks. He might think it was you or me."

"Why you? Sykes was angry with me."

"He was mad at both of us. He thought you dealt me a winning hand."

"I did."

"I mean deliberately."

London smiled.

"How do you know I didn't?"

"I would have noticed."

"Do you think so?"

"I didn't come here to play games, London."

"Okay, okay," London said, "you want me to talk to the sheriff, I'll talk to the sheriff. Hell, I didn't kill Sykes, and neither did you. Let him find out who did. That's his job."

"What about the Sykes brothers?" Clint asked.

"What about them?"

"Are they going to come after us?"

"I don't know," London said. He rubbed his face vigorously, trying to wake himself up. "I guess if they think we killed him they'll come after us. If they do, we'll handle it."

"Maybe the sheriff can head them off for us."

"Hey, we handled four guys the other night, I'm sure we can handle the three Sykes brothers."

Clint didn't bother to point out that it was he who had handled three guys the other night while London had handled one. If not for Clint, London would have been dead.

"If that's all, Clint, I'm gonna get back to bed. I've still got a few hours before it gets to be noon. Tell the sheriff I'll look for him as soon as I get up and have something to eat."

"I'll tell him."

As Clint was leaving the room, London was crawling back into bed. There was another figure under the covers, but it never moved and Clint never saw who it was, or asked.

He debated going back to his own room but knew he'd end up spending hours in bed again with Jenny. Instead he decided to go downstairs and see if he could find some breakfast.

TWENTY-FOUR

Clint couldn't get any breakfast downstairs. Since the hotel was part of the saloon there was no dining room, and while he could have gotten coffee there was no food to be found. He had to go out in the mud for that.

When he got outside he thanked God that at least some of the water had dried up. When he stepped off the platform he realized that it hadn't dried up so much as it had sunk in. Before he was done in Chinaville he was going to need a new pair of boots.

He remembered a small café from his walk the day before and decided to try it. It was a small wood frame building with some tables in the front. They had expanded the back with a tent, and there were many more tables back there, which was where a waiter led him to. The front was full, but the back was less than half full.

"Eggs," Clint said, "scrambled, and whatever you can give me with them."

"Yes, sir."

Clint didn't know what to expect from a café like this in a mining town, so he was surprised when the coffee was good—black and strong—and the eggs came with steak and potatoes, and fresh biscuits.

"Anything else, sir?" the waiter asked.

"No, I think this will do it," Clint said.

While he was eating, he saw a man come in and speak briefly with the waiter, who pointed to him. As the man approached, Clint recognized him as one of the miners he'd played poker with last night. It was the man who had warned him and London that Sykes was a back-shooter.

"Can I sit down?" the man asked.

"Go ahead."

The man sat.

"Want some coffee?"

"Uh, yeah, okay."

Clint signaled the waiter for another cup.

"My name's Ben Newman," the man said. "You're Clint Adams, right?"

"That's right."

"I saw what you did the other night in the saloon."

"I didn't have much choice."

"Sure you did," Newman said as the waiter set an empty cup down in front of him and then filled it. "You coulda let them kill London."

"Like I said, I didn't have much choice."

Newman sipped the coffee and burned his mouth.

"What can I do for you, Mr. Newman? I'm trying to have my breakfast."

Newman put the cup down and spoke with his hand pressed to his bottom lip. He hadn't shaved in several days, maybe a week, and his hair was long and unkempt. Behind all the hair he looked to be in his early thirties.

"I, uh, heard about Harley Sykes."

"So?"

"I just wanted to warn you about his brothers. They'll be comin' after you."

"Why?"

"Huh?"

"Why will they be coming after me?"

"Uh, well, because of Harley."

"Harley's dead, Newman. His brothers will be upset about that, but I still don't know what that has to do with me."

"Well, uh, the word is you killed him."

"Me?"

"Uh, well, you or London."

"Or maybe both of us, huh?"

"Uh, yeah, I guess—"

Clint put down his silverware and stared across the table at the man.

"Do you really think it would take the two of us to shoot Harley Sykes in the back?"

"Uh, I guess not—"

"And do you know of anyone who actually saw us kill Sykes?"

"Well, no—"

Clint picked his silverware back up and said, "I don't think you better finish your coffee, Newman."

"What?"

"I think you better go."

"Huh?"

"Leave!" Clint shouted, attracting the attention of the other diners. "And if I hear that it's you who's been spreading these rumors about me, you better hope I don't see you again."

"Hey," Newman said, "I was just tryin' to help—"

"Do me a favor," Clint said, "don't help me."

"But—"

"Get out, Newman."

Newman stared at Clint for a few moments, then stood up, still fingering his burned lip, and left.

Clint looked down at his half-consumed breakfast and dropped his fork in disgust. The appearance of Newman had ruined his appetite. He poured himself another cup of coffee and sat back with it in hand.

If the word was already out that he and London had killed Harley Sykes, then there was no doubt in his mind that the Sykes brothers would be coming after them.

Unless Virgil Train could dissuade them.

TWENTY-FIVE

Train followed Jakes out to the Sykes claim near Cripple Creek. Two of the brothers were working outside while the third was inside the tunnel. The two outside brothers stopped what they were doing and stared at the two riders. They were shirtless, with chests likes slabs of stone. They looked to be in their early to mid-thirties, both sporting unkempt beards and hair.

As Train and Jakes got closer, the brothers saw the badge on Train's chest and the collar around his neck. They exchanged a glance, and then looked back at Train as he reined in.

"Jakes," one of them said.

"Boys."

"What do you want?"

"Ed, Joe, this is Sheriff Train."

"Sheriff?" Ed asked. "Or Preacher?"

"Both," Train said. "Aren't there three of you?"

"Yeah," Joe said, "Al is in the tunnel."

"You better get him out here," Train said.

"Why?"

"I've got some news that all three of you should hear," Train said. "Why don't you get him?"

The two brothers exchanged another glance, and Train realized that the Sykes brothers weren't too smart.

"Ed," he said, "why don't you fetch Al?"

The decision made for them, Ed said, "Right."

As Ed went off to get their other brother, Joe asked, "What's this about? Harley get into trouble again?"

"Why do you ask that?"

Joe shrugged.

"He didn't come back from town last night."

"He didn't?"

"No."

That meant that he had probably been killed last night, rather than having come back to town in the morning and gotten killed then.

"So?" Joe asked.

"So what?"

"Is this about Harley?"

"Yes, it is."

Train offered no more information, and Joe didn't ask. They all waited until Ed came back with Al. Train wondered about their parents giving them names that could be shortened that way. Was it because they would be easier to remember?

Ed came out of the tunnel with another man trailing him. Al was apparently the oldest—and biggest—

of the brothers. He had the same unkempt hair and beard, but while his brothers had hairless chests his was a mass of wiry gray and black hair. He appeared to be in his early forties. He was glistening with perspiration.

"What's this about, Sheriff?" Al Sykes asked.

"Your brother Harley." Train and Jakes hadn't bothered to dismount. Jakes was grateful for that. The times he'd been around them in the past he'd felt intimidated by their size.

"What about him?"

"He's dead."

All three brothers stared at Train, Al wiping himself down with a rag.

"How?"

"Somebody shot him."

"Who?"

"I don't know."

"Where?"

"In town."

"Where'd you find him?"

"In the alley, next to the Buckhorn Saloon."

Al nodded, wiping his arms.

"What do you want us to do?"

The question surprised Train.

"He's at the undertaker's," Train said. "You might want to see about his burial."

Al nodded again.

"We'll come in later," he said. "We're in the middle of somethin' now."

"You'd do well to get it done today," Train said. "The undertaker will charge you for each day he's got to keep him."

"Okay."

Train sat his horse and stared down at the brothers. Ed and Joe were staring at Al, waiting for some sort of cue.

"Do you have any idea who did it, Sheriff?" Al asked.

Jakes looked at Train.

"No," the sheriff said.

"Was he gambling last night?"

"That's what I hear."

"Probably got into an argument with somebody."

"Maybe."

"Did he or didn't he?"

"I haven't asked around yet, Mr. Sykes," Train said. "I wanted to come out here and tell you about it first."

Al tossed the rag away, put his hands on his hips, and stared up at Train.

"When we bury him," he said, "would you say some words over him, Preacher?"

Train was caught off guard by the request.

"I'd be happy to, Mr. Sykes."

"Much obliged," Sykes said, "and thanks for comin' out to tell us."

"It's my job," Train said. "I guess I'll be seeing you in town."

"Before the day is over," Al said, nodding.

Train returned his nod and turned his horse. Jakes followed, looking back behind them nervously.

TWENTY-SIX

"What are we gonna do?" Ed asked.

Al looked at him, then looked at Joe.

"We'll finish up here and then go into town to take care of Harley."

"How?" Joe asked.

"We're gonna bury him," Al said. "He was our little brother."

"He was a pain in the neck," Ed said. "Him and his gambling."

"His gambling probably got him killed," Joe said. "Little asshole. Now he won't be losing his share of the gold."

Al studied his brothers for a moment, then stepped in and hit each of them on the jaw. Ed got hit with a right that knocked him on his back, and then before he could react Joe got hit with a left and fell on his ass.

"What'd you do that for?" Joe asked, being the first

to recover. Al could hit harder with his right than he could with his left.

"No matter what Harley did, he was still our brother," Al said. "We're gonna bury him and then we're gonna find out who killed him and take care of them."

Both brothers picked themselves up off the ground.

"We got a good thing goin' here, Al," Joe said, "and now we've got an extra share."

"You sayin' you want to forget about Harley?" Al demanded. He was not quite as calm as he'd appeared when Train was there. In fact, he'd been seething even then about his younger brother being killed. "Forget about somebody killin' our brother?"

"We'll do whatever you say, Al," Ed said. "You know that."

"Then you get in the tunnel, Ed," Al said. "We'll finish up here and ride into town to take care of Harley. All right?"

"Right," Ed said.

"All right, Joe?"

"Whatever you say, Al."

"Good," Al said. "Now let's get to work."

Train reined in abruptly. Jakes kept going a few yards before he realized it, and then turned back.

"What's wrong, Sheriff?"

"Tell me about the Sykes brothers, Jakes."

"I don't know them real well, Sheriff."

"But you know them."

"Yeah."

"Are they a close family?"

Jakes shrugged.

"They're brothers."

"There's something bothering me."

"What?"

"They didn't seem upset."

Jakes rubbed a hand over his jaw.

"That was botherin' me, too, Sheriff."

"Why?"

"Well, the times I've seen the brothers they've never been calm about anything. Well, except for Al."

"What about Al?"

"They all follow him. The other three fought among themselves, but never Al. Still, he seemed too calm about his little brother being killed."

"An act," Train said. "It was an act."

"Maybe," Jakes said.

"Let's get back to town," Train said. "I've got to talk to Adams and London. When the Sykes boys get to town they're gonna hear about them."

"Maybe they did it," Jakes said.

Train looked at him and said, "I guess there's always that possibility."

TWENTY-SEVEN

Clint was sitting in a chair in front of the saloon when Train came riding back into town with Jakes. He was hoping to get this cleared up as soon as possible. Maybe London wasn't worried about trouble from the Sykes brothers, but Clint felt he had killed enough people since arriving in Chinaville. He wasn't looking to add any more.

Clint waited for Train to take care of his horse and return to his office. Once the man was inside, Clint got out of his chair and crossed the street.

As Clint entered the office, Train looked up from his desk.

"Have you been watchin' for me?" the lawman asked.

"As a matter of fact, yes," Clint said.

"Have a seat."

Clint sat across from the desk.

"I just came back from seein' the Sykes brothers," Train said.

"And?"

"They took the news very well—too well."

"You don't think they were being honest?"

"One of them wasn't," Train said. "The oldest one, Al. He did all the talkin'."

"And the other two?"

"They're not real smart," Train said. "They'll do whatever Al tells them to do."

"And what's he going to tell them to do?"

"I don't know," Train said. "They'll be coming in later to see about burial plans for their brother."

"What do they know about what happened last night?" Clint asked.

"They figured he had an argument with somebody about a poker game," Train told him, "but they didn't hear about who it was from me. They'll hear that when they get to town."

"Then the question becomes, what will they do about it?"

"I'll keep an eye on them the whole time they're here," Train said.

"What are they like?" Clint asked.

"Big, real big, and not very smart. Al, the oldest, seems to be the smartest."

"What about weapons?"

"I don't know what they have, or how good they are with . . . whatever they have. That's something else I'll find out when they come to town. By the way, did you tell London I wanted to talk to him?"

"I did. He never gets up before noon. After he's

eaten he'll come over and talk to you. I guess that means he'll be here anytime now."

Train nodded, then looked thoughtful for a moment. Clint did not interrupt his thoughts.

"Tell me something, Clint."

"What?"

"Do you think he could have done it?"

"London?"

Train nodded.

"I've only known him for two days, Sheriff," Clint said, "but somehow I don't think he would."

Train nodded.

"Why don't you ask me if I did it?"

"Because I don't think you did."

"Why not?"

"He was shot in the back," Train said. "A man like you would have shot him face-to-face. There'd be no need to do otherwise."

"A man like me?"

Train nodded.

Clint decided to leave without having that statement clarified.

TWENTY-EIGHT

When Clint left the sheriff's office he went back across the street to the Buckhorn Saloon. When he entered, Vince was behind the front desk. He had not yet opened the saloon.

At that point Billy London came down the stairs, looking awake and impeccably dressed.

"Mornin'," he greeted.

Clint and Vince returned the greeting.

"You talk to the sheriff yet?" London asked Clint.

"I did."

"What's he got to say?"

"He thinks there's going to be some trouble from the Sykes brothers."

"Well, we figured on that. How'd they react?"

"Not the way you or I would have if we heard our brother had been killed."

"You got a brother?"

"No."

"Well, I do," London said, "and I'd be plum tickled if I heard he was dead."

Clint waved his hand and said, "I don't think that's a story I want to hear."

"You have breakfast?"

"I did."

"Lunch?"

"Not yet."

"Well, you can have lunch while I have breakfast."

"You're not going to tell me about your brother, are you?"

"Talk about that son of a bitch?" London said. "Not a chance."

"Okay, then."

"Let's go down the street to the café."

"Suits me. That's where I ate this morning."

"I can make some sandwiches," Vince said.

"If I remember right, your sandwiches were a little dry," Clint said.

"Suited you yesterday."

"That was yesterday. We'll see you later, Vince."

Clint and London walked out of the saloon and started toward the café.

"Are the Sykes boys in town yet?" London asked.

"No, not yet. Sheriff said they'd be coming in later."

"Good, that means we can eat without interruption."

"I told the sheriff you'd talk to him after you ate," Clint said.

"Oh, I will, don't worry. I won't make a liar out of you."

They reached the café and went inside. It was busier now than when Clint was here earlier, but they were still shown to a table in the back section.

"Eggs," London said, "and biscuits."

"Anything else?" the waiter asked.

"Just coffee."

"No potatoes, no bacon, no ham?"

"No nothin'," London said. "Just eggs, biscuits, and coffee."

"Okay," the waiter said, with a shrug. "How about you?"

"Coffee and a sandwich," Clint said.

"What kind of sandwich?"

"Surprise me."

The waiter shook his head and said, "Okay."

"Eggs and nothing else?" Clint asked.

"I'm having biscuits. That's good enough. I don't eat a lot, is all."

"Well, I had breakfast, so I'm just having a sandwich."

"Now that we got our diet straight, what do you figure to do?"

"About what?"

"About the Sykes brothers. You gonna ride out?"

"Why would I ride out? I haven't finished what I came here to do."

"You won a bit last night."

"You took five dollars of it away from me," Clint said. "I'm not leaving until I get that five dollars back."

"Fair enough."

"Besides, I can't leave you to face those boys

alone. It looks to me like you can only handle one at a time."

"Is that a fact? I'll have you know I could have handled two of those fellows."

"And the other two would have killed you. Why don't you carry a bigger gun?"

"Well, I don't expect every poker game to turn into a shoot-out. I can usually hit what I aim at with this." He raised his hand to indicate the derringer that he was wearing on his wrist.

"Well, you've managed to stay alive—what, forty years?"

"Thirty-five." London touched his face, looking insulted.

The waiter brought the food over and set it in front of them.

"What is that?" Clint asked, pointing to his sandwich.

"Chicken."

Clint lifted the bread and said, "Looks dry."

"I can bring you some butter."

Clint made a face and said, "Never mind. I'll wash it down with coffee."

The waiter shrugged and walked away.

"I guess we better eat and stop talkin'," London said. "You aren't gonna be able to say much with a mouthful of dry sandwich."

Clint had taken a bite already and couldn't talk, so he just nodded.

TWENTY-NINE

After their meal they left the café and stepped outside.

"I guess I better go and talk to the sheriff," London
said.

"That would be nice," Clint said. "After all, you
wouldn't want to make a liar out of me."

"No, I sure wouldn't. What are you gonna do?"

"I guess I'll go over to the saloon."

"I'll see you there."

Clint watched London cross the street and head
off for the jail, and he started for the saloon.

Virgil Train was pouring himself a cup of coffee
when London walked into his office.

"Sheriff."

"Afternoon, Mr. London. Nice of you to come over
and see me."

116

"Clint told you I'd be here," London said. "I wouldn't want to make a liar out of him."

"Coffee?"

"Sure, why not?"

Train handed London the cup he'd already poured and then poured himself another one.

"Where were you last night, Mr. London?"

"You mean when Harley Sykes was gettin' himself killed?"

"That's what I mean."

"I was in bed."

"Alone?"

"Well, this may offend the preacher in you, Sheriff," London said, "but I wasn't alone, no. I had a lady in bed with me."

Train gave him a momentary look of disapproval and then sat down behind his desk.

"One of the girls from the saloon?"

"That's right."

"Which one?"

"Maude, the redhead. You can ask her, she'll tell you."

"I'll ask her."

"You really think I killed that man, Sheriff?"

"To tell you the truth, Mr. London," Train said, "I'm just not sure."

"Well, that sure is honest."

"I'm just doin' my job, Mr. London."

"Well, Sheriff, can you see any reason why I shouldn't keep on doin' mine?"

"No, I don't," Train said. "Just don't leave town—and try not to shoot anybody."

London stood up and said, "I'll give it my best shot."

He waited long enough to see that the joke was lost on Train, then left.

THIRTY

The Sykes brothers rode into town at dusk. Al rode in front, with Ed and Joe riding abreast behind him. They were all wearing worn shirts and Levis. Their saddles were as worn as their clothes, and their horses weren't much better. Al was wearing a big Walker Colt in a holster, and had a rifle in a faded scabbard. Joe was carrying a rifle across his lap, while Ed—who couldn't hit the side of a mountain with a handgun or a rifle—was carrying a shotgun.

Train was walking down the street, making his rounds, and when he saw them ride inhe stepped into the street so they could see him.

They rode up to him and stopped.

"Where's the undertaker's office, Sheriff?" Al asked.

"If you'll all dismount I'll show you."

They stepped down from their horses, taking their weapons with them. Train thought about demanding their guns, but that might start trouble. Better to see what they were going to do first. Besides, everyone else in town was carrying weapons.

"This way."

Train led them across the street to the undertaker's and let them go in ahead of him. Tom Shumaker, the undertaker, recognized the three brothers immediately. They bore a striking resemblance to the dead Harley Sykes.

"You have my condolences," Shumaker said.

"Where is our brother?"

"This way."

Train decided to wait there while Shumaker led the three of them into the back, where their brother was laid out.

When they came out he knew by the set of Al Sykes's jaw that the man was barely keeping control of himself.

"He was shot in the back," Al said.

"I know."

"You didn't tell us that."

"I'm sorry."

"And he was found facedown in the mud?"

Train looked past the Sykes brothers at Shumaker, who looked away.

"That's right."

"Even if he was alive after he was shot he would have drowned in the mud."

"I guess so."

Train saw that Ed and Joe were looking around the room, and not even at each other.

"Al . . ." Train said.

"Have you found out anything yet about who might have killed him?"

"Not really."

"What do you mean, not really?"

"I've questioned some of the people who were in the saloon the night before, but I really don't suspect anyone yet." That was a half-truth. He *had* questioned some of the men who'd been in the saloon, but he did have a suspect. Billy London still looked pretty good for it.

"Sheriff," Al Sykes asked, "who did he play poker with the night before? Who did he have an argument with?"

Train decided to answer because he knew they could find out from someone else.

"He was playing with a couple of other miners, a man named Clint Adams, and the gambler, Billy London."

"London," Joe said. "He played with him before."

"What was the fight about?" Ed asked. Suddenly the other brothers were getting involved.

"Your brother thought he'd been cheated."

"By who?" Al asked.

"I don't know all the details of the game," Train said. "I wasn't there."

"Then we'll have to find out from someone who was there," Al said.

"I don't want any trouble, Al," Train said.

"We just want to know who killed our brother, Sheriff," Al said, "that's all." He looked at Shumaker and asked, "Did we pay you enough?"

"Oh, yes, sir," Shumaker said, "I'll see to the burial myself."

"Much obliged."

Al started for the door with his brothers following.

"I'll tell all three of you again, I don't want any trouble."

Al stopped short and pointed his index finger at Train. For a moment the lawman thought the other man was going to blow up.

"Point that finger somewhere else, Sykes," Train said slowly.

They matched stares for a few moments, and then Al Sykes moved his finger away and stalked out the door without another word. The brothers, Ed and Joe, followed Al out the door without looking at Train.

"What did they pay for, Tom?" Train asked.

"The bare minimum, Sheriff," Shumaker said. "Just a pine box."

"Think they could have afforded more?"

"They have a decent claim, the way I heard it."

"Why would they care so little about his remains, yet want to know who killed him?" Train asked. It was the preacher talking, not the sheriff.

"I don't know, Sheriff," Shumaker said. "It's questions like that make me glad I deal with the dead, and not the living."

THIRTY-ONE

The Sykes brothers walked across the street to get their horses and started walking them over to the livery stable.

"What are we going to do, Al?" Joe asked.

"Well, for one thing we're gonna stay in town until we find out who killed Harley."

"What? What about our claim?" Ed asked.

"It'll still be there."

"Why do we all have to stay?" Joe asked.

"Harley's a pain in the butt even dead," Ed said.

Al turned on them quickly and they both stepped away, thinking he was going to hit them.

"We're brothers," he said to them. "If somebody killed me, I hope you boys would want to find out who did it."

"Well, yeah," Ed said.

"Sure," Joe said.

"But you ain't a pain in the butt."

"It don't matter," Al said. "He was our brother and we're gonna find out who killed him. Understand?"

"Yeah," Ed said.

"Okay," Joe said.

"Here," Al said, handing the reins of his horse to Ed. "You boys get the horses taken care of and I'll try to find someplace for us to stay."

"Where should we meet you?"

"At the saloon."

"Good," Ed said, "after seeing Harley I could use a drink."

"We're not gettin' drunk," Al said. "Remember that."

"Then what are we gonna do at the saloon?" Ed asked.

"We're gonna talk to that gambler, London. He's been taking Harley's gold for a long time now."

"What about the other fellers?" Joe asked.

"We'll have to find out who the other miners were," Al said.

"And the other man? His name sounds familiar," Ed said. "Who's he?"

"His name should sound familiar," Al said. "Clint Adams is the Gunsmith."

"The Gunsmith!" Ed said. "Jesus! We got to face the Gunsmith?"

"What was Harley thinkin'?" Joe demanded. "Why was he playin' poker with the Gunsmith?"

"I don't know," Al said, "but we're gonna find out—but nobody braces Adams alone. Understand?"

"Oh, yeah," Joe said, with enthusiasm.

"I ain't facin' him," Ed said.

"If he killed Harley we'll face him, but we'll do it together."

"J-just the three of us?" Joe asked.

"No," Al said, "that's the other thing I'm gonna do while we're in town."

"What?" Ed asked.

"I'm gonna talk to Bannister."

"Cousin Bannister?" Joe asked.

"If you tell him about the Gunsmith, he'll *want* to face him." Ed saw this as his way out of possibly facing Clint Adams, even with his brothers.

"That's not what I want," Al said. "If we have to face Adams, I'd want Bannister to be there with us, but we'd all do it."

Joe and Ed exchanged a dubious glance.

"Go ahead, take care of the horses and meet me later. Go!"

"We're goin'," Ed said, and he and Joe went off toward the livery stable, leading the three horses.

Al Sykes watched his brothers for a few moments, then turned and walked the other way. Their cousin Bannister had come to Chinaville with them, but after the first few weeks of hard work had decided that gold mining was not for him. Before that he had made his way with a gun, and after that he went back to it. If it came to pass that Clint Adams had killed Harley, Bannister would stand with them and give them more than a fighting chance.

THIRTY-TWO

Sheriff Virgil Train left the undertaker's office soon after the Sykes brothers did. He watched them until they split up. Joe and Ed were apparently taking the horses to the livery stable, while Al was going someplace else.

After the brothers split up, Train walked over to the saloon to find Clint Adams and Billy London.

Clint was standing at the bar when the sheriff entered the saloon. He had returned to the saloon and found Jenny. He felt badly about leaving her that morning, so they went to her room so he could make it up to her. That was where he had spent the past hour, which he was now fondly remembering . . .

Jenny was carefree and inventive in bed, ready to try anything. What he remembered the most was when she got on her knees and held onto the bedposts, presenting him with her delectable rear.

He had moved in behind her and slid his fingers between her thighs. He found her wet and ready and slid one finger into her while he stroked her clit with another.

"Oooh, you got me burning and wet, Clint," she said. "Come on, come on . . ."

He knew what she wanted, so he removed his finger, got closer to her, and this time slid his penis between her thighs and plunged into her. She arched her back and gasped, and he took hold of her hips and began to move in and out of her that way . . .

He looked around quickly, as if he thought someone might be able to tell what he was thinking. To dispel the thoughts of sex with Jenny, who was now working, he looked around the room.

Billy London was sitting at his table, a game in session. Clint had come in too late and there was not an open chair. He found this interesting. London had held a chair for him the day before, all protests aside. Today he had not. Clint chose to believe that he had cost London some money yesterday by playing in his game. Today London wanted to get a bit of a head start. By the time a chair finally opened up the gambler should be significantly ahead.

Clint saw Train enter, and when the lawman spotted him he raised his beer mug to him.

"Can I buy you a beer, Sheriff?" Clint asked as the man reached him.

"Sure, why not?"

While waiting, Train checked to make sure London was at his table.

"He hasn't gone anywhere," Clint said.

"Why aren't you playin'?"

"No room at the table," Clint said. "Maybe later."

Vince brought the sheriff's beer, and Train picked it up and turned his back to the bar, leaning on it.

He took a sip of beer and said, "I just saw the Sykes brothers."

"Saw, or talked to?"

"Both. They were over at the undertaker's."

"How'd they react?"

"I hadn't told them that he was shot in the back or the way he was found."

"Didn't take it well, huh?"

Train looked at Clint, who could see the confusion on the man's face.

"I don't understand these people," Train said. "They don't seem to care much that their brother is dead, just that somebody killed him."

"And that confuses you, huh, Preacher?"

"Yes, doesn't it confuse you?"

"No, not really."

"Then explain it to me."

"How about I do that after you tell me the rest of it?" Clint suggested.

"Well, I just don't know what these men are gonna do," Train said. "The older one, Al, he's very quiet, but very intense."

"Did you take their guns?"

Train hesitated, then said, "No."

"You should have taken their guns."

"I wouldn't want anyone trying to take my gun in a town like this," Train said.

"Now you're not talking like a lawman or a preacher, Preacher," Clint said.

"Who am I talkin' like?"

"Like . . . well, like me. I wouldn't want to be in this town without a gun, either, but the fact is you should have taken their guns."

Train took a long drink and then said, "I guess I wasn't cut out to be a lawman."

"And what about bein' a preacher?"

"I think I'm good at that."

"Maybe you could have preached their guns away from them."

"I just didn't think they'd give their weapons up easily."

"They wouldn't have, but . . ."

"Okay, okay, I take your point," Train said. "It's likely that they'll make trouble, so I should have disarmed them."

"Right. What kind of weapons do they have?"

"Al's wearing a side arm, but not the others. One's got a rifle and the other a shotgun."

"Al wear the pistol like he knows how to use it?"

"I'd say yes," Train said. "It's worn, it's been used, but he keeps it clean."

"Well, my advice would be to keep an eye on them."

"I intend to."

"Did you, uh, tell them about the game? And the argument?"

"I did," Train said. "I figured they'd hear about it somewhere else, anyway."

"You were right about that. I guess this means London and I will be hearing from them."

"Definitely. Listen, Clint—"

"I know what you're going to say," Clint said. "Try not to shoot any of them."

"Unless they try to shoot you first."

"Why, Sheriff," Clint said, "it's kind of you to add that."

THIRTY-THREE

Clint and Train finished their beers watching the activity in the saloon. Jenny caught sight of Clint from across the room and smiled.

"Is Jenny the woman you . . . were with last night?"

"Yes. Do you want to ask her?"

Train thought a moment and then shook his head.

"No, it won't be necessary."

"Thanks for that."

"Who was with London?"

"Why are you ready to believe that London did it and not me?"

"Clint, you've killed a lot of men in your time—maybe not as many as your reputation says, but more than a few. Isn't that so?"

Clint hesitated only a second before he said, "Yes."

"I don't recall your shootin' any of them in the back," Train said.

"I never did."

"I know, but I don't know that about him . . . do you?"

Clint had to answer frankly. "No, I don't."

"Do you know who the girl was?"

"No, I don't," Clint said. "I guess you'll have to ask him."

"I guess so."

Clint smiled, patted Train on the back, and said, "You're really not cut out to be a lawman, are you?"

Train looked at him and said, "How do I get them to listen to me, Clint? When I want to tell them about God? How do I do that without the badge?"

"If they listen to you now, Virgil, isn't it because they're afraid of you?"

"I suppose so."

"If you didn't have that badge, and the gun, and you talked to them in a church, I think they'd listen."

The word Virgil Train heard was "church." It didn't dawn on him until several moments later that Clint talked about him taking off his gun.

"A church," Train said. "This town doesn't have a church."

"Build one," Clint said.

"That's something I'll have to think about."

"Build a church, Virgil," Clint said, "and be a preacher full-time."

Train had two thoughts in mind. One, could he build a church here? And two, could he put down his gun?

THIRTY-FOUR

Al Sykes found his cousin, Bannister Smith, in a whore's crib at the far south end of town. Al knew that he'd find Bannister with a whore, so he just started hitting the lowest ones, the ones working out of tents. It wasn't that Bannister couldn't afford some of the better whores in the saloons. He actually liked the cheap whores.

"Bannister?" Sykes called from outside the tent.

"What? Who's that?" a gruff voice called out.

"It's Al. Bannister?"

"Al who?"

"Sykes," Al Sykes said, "your cousin."

"Al? What the hell ya want?"

"I wanna talk to you," Sykes shouted. "Come on out, damn it."

Sykes heard a woman squeak from inside the tent, and then Bannister appeared at the tent flap, naked. He held the tent flap back so that Sykes was able to see the woman. She was chubby, with big, floppy breasts and a roll of flesh around her waist. Sykes knew that his cousin liked big, fleshy women, and she certainly fit that description. She had apparently just regained her feet and was rubbing her big butt.

"Ya didn't have ta dump me like that!" the woman called from inside.

Bannister Smith was a big man, almost as big as Al Sykes. They were born within a month of each other, and had been very close since that time—which did not mean that they didn't fight. They'd had more knock-down fights than either could remember, and had each taken turns being the winner.

Naked, Bannister Smith looked like he was covered with hair, and his erect penis jutted up from a dark forest of hair between his legs.

"I've told you, by God, never to try to tell me what to—" Bannister bellowed, but Sykes interrupted him.

"Harley's dead, Bannister!"

Bannister Smith stopped short and then asked, "What?" His bushy eyebrows knit together. "Harley?"

"Dead," Sykes said. "Somebody shot him in the back."

"Who?"

"We don't know, but we're gonna find out. We may need you."

Although Al Sykes and Bannister Smith were pretty evenly matched physically, Bannister had one major advantage—he was good with a gun.

He was very good with a gun.

"For what?"

"Clint Adams is in town."

"Clint Adams . . . the Gunsmith?"

"That's right."

"Let me get my gun," Smith said, starting to go back into the tent.

"Wait, wait, wait," Sykes said, grabbing his cousin's arm.

"What?"

"Adams may not have killed him."

"Who else?"

"A gambler named London."

"Billy London?"

"You know him. He's got a table at the saloon."

"Yeah, I know him."

"Harley played poker with them last night before he was killed," Sykes said, "but there were two other miners in the game. We've got to find out who they were, too."

"Whataya want me to do?"

"Stay where I can find you."

"I'll be right here."

"If it's Adams, do you want—"

"If it's Adams," Bannister Smith said, "I want."

"Okay."

Smith went back into the tent, and Sykes heard the girl squeal again.

Sykes turned and walked away from the girl's crib. He didn't know why Bannister liked these girls. He was likely to catch something from them that would stay with him for a long time, or kill him.

Sykes just hoped that he wouldn't die before he helped them.

THIRTY-FIVE

A chair opened at London's game, and Clint was about to go over and take it when Virgil Train grabbed his arm.

"Wha—"

"The door."

Clint looked and saw two big men with bushy hair and beards enter.

"They look like Sykes boys," Clint said.

"They are," Train said. "Joe and Ed."

"Where's big brother Al?" Clint wondered.

"I don't know," Train said, "but they're probably gonna meet him here."

"Here is not a good place," Clint said.

"You go and play your game," Train said. "I'll keep an eye on the boys."

"Preach to them, Preacher."

"I'll preach to them," Train said, "and then I'll preach to you."

"A lot of good that'll do you," Clint said, and walked over to London's table to take the empty seat.

"Welcome to the game," London said. He was looking down at the table, stacking his money.

"A couple of friends of yours just walked in, London."

"Oh yeah?" London looked at him. "Who?"

"Just moving toward the bar now."

London took a look, then turned his eyes to Clint again.

"Sykes?"

"Just two of them," Clint said. "Train figures they're here waiting for older brother Al."

"And then what?"

"And then we'll just have to see."

"Are we gonna play poker?" one of the other players asked.

"We're gonna play cards," London said. "Whose deal is it?"

Joe and Ed Sykes went right to the bar and ordered a beer each.

"I don't see Al," Joe said.

"If he was here he'd be at the bar," Ed said.

They picked up their beers and turned to face the room.

"Which one is that gambler, London?" Joe asked.

Ed looked around the room and then said, "I don't remember. Harley was the one who played with him, not you or me."

"Or me."

"I said that."

"Oh."

"Al will know."

"Where is Al, anyway?"

"He'll be here," Ed said. "He's got to find Bannister first."

Joe laughed and said, "We know where Bannister's gonna be, huh?"

"Yeah," Ed said, laughing, "down by the cribs."

They both laughed, and then Ed stopped and nudged his brother.

"What?"

"That's that weird sheriff, ain't it?"

Joe turned his head to the left to take a look, then turned back to his brother.

"Yeah, the one who wears a preacher's collar."

"He's watchin' us."

"We ain't doin' nothin' but havin' a beer," Joe said.

"I know that, but he's still watchin' us."

"So what do we do?"

"Nothin'," Ed said, "we don't do nothin' until Al gets here."

"Maybe he'll have Bannister with him," Joe said. "Maybe he'll kill that sheriff."

"That'd be stupid," Ed said.

"Don't call me stupid."

"I didn't say you were stupid," Ed said, "I said killin' a lawman would be stupid. Al says we're after whoever killed Harley, and that's all."

"Well, I wish Al would get here already," Joe said.

"Yeah," Ed agreed, "so do I."

THIRTY-SIX

Train watched the brothers for a few moments, then decided to walk over to them. They had each laid their weapons down on the floor, leaning up against the bar, and they each had a beer mug in their hands.

"You boys are missin' somebody," Train said.

"Huh?" Joe said.

"Who?" Ed asked.

"Al," Train said. "Where's your older brother tonight?"

"He's, uh, he's . . ." Joe stammered.

"We don't know," Ed said.

"Yeah," Joe chimed in, "we don't know."

"You boys find a place to spend the night?" Train asked.

"Oh, no, not yet," Joe said.

"That's what Al's tryin' to do," Ed said, as if it had

just occurred to him. "He's tryin' to find us a place to stay."

"The town's pretty full up," Train said. "You might not find a place."

Ed and Joe simply exchanged a glance.

"Might have to sleep in a barn."

"I slept in a barn before," Joe said. "It was comfortable. Lots of hay."

"Shut up," Ed said.

"You might even have to go back to your claim."

Again the brothers exchanged a glance, not knowing what to say, but they were saved from further embarrassment by the appearance of Al Sykes.

The elder Sykes stepped through the batwing doors and spotted his brothers talking to Sheriff Train.

"Are you botherin' my brothers, Sheriff?" he said, approaching them.

"Why, no, sir, I'm not. Am I, boys?"

"Well . . ." Joe said.

"Shut up, Joe."

"Quit tellin' me to shut up," Joe said.

"Did you find a place for you and your brothers to stay, Al?" Train asked.

"As a matter of fact, yeah, I did, Sheriff."

"Well, that's good."

"You mind if me and my brothers have a beer, Sheriff?" Al asked.

"Well, no, Al, I don't mind that at all."

"And we might just have us a conversation with Billy London and Clint Adams while we're here."

"Just a conversation, Al?"

"We ain't gonna try nothin' while you're here, are we, Sheriff? We ain't that dumb."

"I hope not, Al," Train said, backing off, "I hope not." He went back to his place at the bar.

"What did you boys tell him?" Al asked.

"We didn't tell him nothin', Al," Joe said.

Al asked for and got a beer, and turned to face his brothers.

"Did you find Bannister?" Ed asked.

"I found him."

"Then how come he ain't with you?" Joe asked.

"Because we don't need him just yet, Joe."

"But he is gonna help us?" Ed asked. "I mean, if we have to face Adams?"

"Yeah, he's gonna help."

"Al, which one is Billy London?"

Al looked around and said, "That little feller over there."

"And what about Adams?" Joe asked.

"Is that him at the table?" Ed asked.

"I don't know," Al said, "but there's one way to find out. Come on."

"Wait . . ." Both brothers started to pick up their weapons.

"Leave those here," Al said.

"Leave 'em?" Ed asked.

"But, Al—" Joe said.

"We won't need 'em," Al said. "We're just gonna talk—for now."

THIRTY-SEVEN

Train saw the three Sykes brothers start for London's table. His first instinct was to move to intercept, but then he noticed that Joe and Ed Sykes had left their weapons leaning against the bar. Train leaned back against the bar and settled down to watch.

Clint was watching the Sykes brothers from the corner of his eye, and when he saw them start toward the table he said, "Let's be alert, London."

London, studying his opponent's cards on the table, said, "They most likely just want to talk, Clint."

"Yeah," Clint said, "this time."

"Is this about Harley?" one of the other players asked. He was a miner who knew the Sykes brothers.

"Jesus," another man said, "I'm gonna fold and get out of here."

"You are high man on the table, sir," London said. "You'd be a fool to fold."

"I'd be a fool to stay here and get shot," the man said.

"Nobody is going to get shot," London said. "Just sit quietly, gentlemen, and we'll be able to get back to the game momentarily."

With that London looked up and smiled as the three Sykes brothers arrived at the table.

Al did the talking while Joe and Ed just watched.

"Are you London?"

"I am," London said.

Al Sykes looked at Clint.

"And you're Clint Adams?"

"I am."

"You played poker with our brother, Harley, the other night."

"We played poker *against* your brother," London said. "What of it?"

"I heard there was an argument."

"A minor one."

"What about?"

"Your brother was a bad card player," London said. Clint decided that since they were at London's table he'd let the man take the lead. "He claimed that he was cheated."

"Harley *was* a bad poker player," Al said, "but that ain't nothin' to die over."

"If you have a question you want to ask me, Mr. Sykes," London said, "ask away."

"Did you shoot my brother in the back?"

"No, I did not."

The elder Sykes looked at Adams.

"Did you?"

"I didn't."

"If either of you did," he said, "you'd lie to me, anyway."

"Probably," London said.

"No," Clint said, "I wouldn't."

"Why not?" Al asked.

"Because if I thought your brother did something to deserve to die, and I killed him, I would tell you."

"But would you have shot him in the back?"

"That's not my style, Mr. Sykes. No, I would not have shot him in the back."

"Your brother accused me of cheating, Sykes," London said. "He's lucky I didn't kill him on the spot."

"Maybe you just waited and did it later."

"No," London said, "if I thought he deserved to die I would have killed him on the spot."

The three brothers stood there for a moment in silence. Ed and Joe were looking around the room, but Al was studying Clint and London, trying to figure out which one was lying.

"If there's nothing else, Sykes," London said, "I have a game going here."

"There's nothin' else," Al Sykes said, "not now, anyway."

"In the event you want to talk to me again," London said, "I'm at your disposal."

"Huh?" Ed said.

"We'll be here if you want to talk again," Clint said.

"We just might do that," Al said. He turned to his brothers and said, "Get your guns. We're leavin'."

Al turned and walked out of the saloon without another word. Joe and Ed scrambled for their guns and followed their brother out.

The other three players at the table let out their breaths.

"That was close," one of them said.

"Think he believed ya?" another miner asked.

"Better hope he believed it," the third man said. "Them Sykes boys can be a mean bunch—and they got a cousin in town who's worse than all three."

"A cousin?" Clint asked. "Who?"

"Name's Bannister Smith."

"Smith is cousin to the Sykes brothers?" Clint asked, surprised. He knew the name.

"That's right," the third miner said, "and he's in town."

"London," Clint said, "we have to talk."

"We can talk later," London said, "right now, gentlemen, we have a card game to play."

THIRTY-EIGHT

Clint was losing, and it was because he wasn't concentrating, not because Billy London was ultimately a better poker player than he was. In point of fact, the man seemed to have better concentration, which probably did—in the long run—make him a better player.

"That's it, gents," Clint said. "I'm done for the night."

"Bad run of luck," one of the miners said.

London caught Clint's eye and shook his head slightly. He knew it was not a run of bad luck.

"See you later," London said.

"Right."

Clint got up and went to the bar. He was surprised to see that Virgil Train was still there. The man looked odd leaning against the bar with his gun, his badge, and his clerical collar. Also, he seemed to be drunk.

"You still here?"

"I made some rounds, but I came back," Train said. "Did the game go badly for you tonight?"

"I can't seem to concentrate."

"Why not?"

"I keep thinking about Harley Sykes."

"Why?"

"Well, the whole saloon heard him threaten me and London, right?"

"Right."

"If there was someone in the saloon who had something against him, wouldn't that night be a perfect time to kill him? London and I would be the prime suspects."

"I follow you. What you're sayin' is that the killer was in the saloon that night."

"Right."

"So all I got to do is question everybody who was in the saloon until I find the guilty man and he confesses. Sounds easy."

"What about the other men who were playing poker with us? The other two miners?"

"Who were they?"

"I don't know. Maybe London remembers their— wait a minute. I remember one of them."

"Who?"

"A man named Newman."

"Newman," Train said, frowning. "I know Newman. He's not a miner."

"He's not?"

"Well, he was, but his claim dried up."

"When was that?"

"Oh, a month or so ago. Why?"

Clint told Train about Newman coming to see him.

"He seemed intent on trying to convince me that the Sykes were going to come after me and London."

"So he thinks you or London did it?"

"He seemed real anxious to pit us against the Sykes brothers," Clint said. "I wonder why."

"Maybe we should ask him."

"Do you know where he lives?"

"No."

"Then we have to look for him," Clint said, "unless London knows."

"Well," Train said, putting his beer mug down on the bar, "you can ask London tonight, and then we'll find Newman and ask him tomorrow."

"Where are you going?" Clint asked.

"To my office," Train said. "I've got a lot of thinkin' to do."

"About what?"

Train stared at Clint, who saw that the man's eyes were not clear, as they had been every other time he'd talked to him, but bloodshot.

"Guns, churches, badges," Train said, with a wave of his hand. "Lots of things. Just things."

"Can you make it?"

"I'll make it," Train said. "I'll see you in the morning."

Clint watched as the tall man walked unsteadily to the door. Without letting Train know, he followed him out, then trailed him until he entered his office. Anyone seeing the unsteady condition of the man might have thought it was an ideal time to try him.

No matter how Virgil Train tried to change his life—
lawman, preacher, whatever—he was always going
to carry that reputation with him. Clint knew this
from personal experience. He'd tried many times to
get away from his reputation, and it never worked.
He knew if he ever put his gun down, he'd be dead.

But maybe Virgil Train had a chance. Maybe if he
got himself a church and became a real preacher
he'd be able to put his guns away. Who knew what
would happen if he became a real cleric, no gun, no
badge?

Clint turned and walked back to the saloon.

After the Sykes brothers left the saloon, Joe and
Ed caught up to Al.

"Where are we staying?" Joe asked.

"I don't know."

"But you told the sheriff we had a place," Ed said,
confused.

"I lied."

"Why?"

Al ignored the question. He wasn't sure why he
had lied.

"But where are we gonna sleep?"

"I don't know!" Al snapped. "I'm not worried about
where we're gonna sleep. I'm thinkin' about that
gambler."

"What about him?" Joe asked.

"Well, whether he killed Harley or not he sure took
a lot of Harley's gold."

"So?" Ed asked.

"Well, he deserves to have somethin' happen to
him."

"Like what?" Joe asked. "Killin' him?"

"Not until we know that he actually did kill Harley," Al said.

"Then what are ya talkin' about, Al?" Ed asked.

Al remained silent for a moment, then said, "When I figure that out I'll let you know."

"But where are we gonna sleep?" Joe asked plaintively.

"Shut up," Ed said.

THIRTY-NINE

Clint waited in the saloon for London to finish his game. He stood mostly at the bar, talking to Vince, but toward the end of the night, when the place started to empty, he took a corner table and sat with Jenny.

At one point Bennett came over, the game at his table having broken up before the others.

"You seem to have got pretty tight with London," he said.

"I just enjoy playing against him."

"Think I'd be too hard to beat, huh?" Bennett's voice sounded hopeful.

"Yeah, Bennett," he said, "that's right, you're just too damn hard to beat."

Bennett stared at Clint for a moment, then backed away, saying, "Aw, you're just sayin' that." He turned and walked away.

"Were you just sayin' that?" Jenny asked.

"Yes," Clint said. "He's not in London's class."

"Or yours?"

Clint looked at her and smiled.

"That would be immodest of me to say."

"And you wouldn't want to be immodest, would you?" she asked.

"No," he said, "I wouldn't."

"Aw," she said, "you're just sayin' that."

When the game at London's table was over, he came over to Clint and Jenny, carrying a beer.

"Mind if I join you?"

"No," Clint said. "I've been waiting for you."

"Why?"

"I wanted to ask you about the other two men who were playing poker with us last night."

"Is that what you've been thinkin' about all night," London asked, "to the absolute detriment of your poker game?"

"That's it."

"Well, then," London said, "if you've got questions, ask 'em."

"I'll leave you two gentlemen to your questions and answers," Jenny said, standing up, "and I'll say good night."

Both men stood until she walked away, and then sat down.

"Now," London asked, "what's so all-fired important?"

"The other two players last night."

London thought a moment, then said, "Newman and . . . Carpenter."

"Train told me about Newman. His claim went dry. What about Carpenter?"

"He's still working his claim, as far as I know. Why are you interested in them?"

"Because either of them could have killed Sykes last night."

"Why? Because they played poker with him? By the same token you or I could have done it."

"Except that we have already ruled ourselves out . . . right?"

"Right. I know that I didn't do it."

"And I know that I didn't do it."

They stared at each other for a few moments.

"I know you didn't do it," Clint said.

London sat forward in his chair.

"How do you know that?"

"I don't believe you would shoot a man in the back," Clint said.

"But I would," London said.

"What?"

"If I had to shoot a man in the back to save my life, I would. Wouldn't you?"

"Why would I have to shoot a man in the back to save my life?"

London stared at Clint for a few moments, then sat back in his chair.

"No, you wouldn't know that feeling, would you? That fear?"

"Nothing justifies back-shooting," Clint said.

"Maybe not in your world," London said.

"Have you . . . done this already?" Clint asked.

"No, I never have."

"Then not last night?"

"No, not last night," London said. "I'm just tellin' you that I would . . . if I ever had to . . . I would."

"All right."

London drank half his beer and set the mug down carefully on the table.

"It might be interesting to know," Clint said, "what happened to Newman after his claim dried up."

"What do you mean?"

"I mean what he did afterward, what he does now to live, and where he lives. He came to me and tried to convince me that you and I would have to go against the Sykes brothers."

"He wants them to kill us?" London asked.

"Or he wants us to kill them."

"Or each other."

Clint pointed his finger at London and said, "Yes, that must be it."

"But why?"

"If we kill the Sykes brothers," Clint asked, "what happens to their claim?"

London shrugged and said, "Someone else can claim it, I guess."

"Like Newman."

"That son of a bitch," London said. "He killed Harley Sykes to set us against each other."

"Maybe," Clint said.

"Carpenter had no motive."

"What about someone else in the saloon that night?"

"No," London said, shaking his head, "you've got this figured out, Clint. It's Newman."

"Train is going to help me find him tomorrow."

"What a strange man that one is," London said. "You seem to have become fairly good friends in a short time."

"Like you and me?"

London smiled.

"Are we friends?"

"I think we are."

"Then we are," London said. "Do you want me to come with you tomorrow to find Newman?"

"It's up to you," Clint said. "I don't know how well you get along with Train. Also, I don't think he and I want to wait until after noon."

"Well, if that's the case," London said, standing up, "wake me when you find him."

"Good night, London."

London bade Clint good night with a wave of his hand and went up to his room. Vince walked over to Clint's table.

"Want another beer, Clint?"

"I'll just finish this one, Vince," Clint said, "and go to bed."

"Good night, then."

Clint raised his mug in good night, then drank some of its contents. It was by no means a certainty that Newman was the killer, but it was clear that the next logical step was to find him and confront him.

FORTY

When Billy London entered his room he felt the breeze from the window as it caused the curtains to billow about. Too late, he realized that he had not left his window open when he left his room.

He turned quickly to leave the room, but powerful arms caught him from behind and held him. The hold was so tight he almost couldn't breathe.

"He's got a hide-out gun in his sleeve," Al Sykes said. He grabbed London's arm himself and liberated the derringer. He tossed it on the other side of the room.

"Turn up the light, Ed."

Ed Sykes turned the lamp flame higher so London could see him and his brother Al. That meant it was Joe who was holding him.

"This is a much smaller room with you fellas in it," London observed.

Al stepped in and slapped London across the face openhanded.

"You talk only when I ask you a question. Understand?" he asked.

London didn't answer.

Al slapped him.

"I asked you a question."

London sucked on his bloody lip and said, "Yeah, I understand."

"Did you kill our brother, Harley?"

"How did he get the name Harley," London asked, "when you guys are named Al, Ed, and Joe?"

This time Al Sykes backhanded him. London's lips split in two different places, and he felt with his tongue that two of his teeth were loose.

"Did you kill our brother?"

"No."

"Why should I believe you?"

"Hell, man," London said, lisping a bit, "you asked me and I got two choices, yes or no. You got two choices, to believe me or not."

"Well, I choose not," Sykes said, "so I'll ask again." He hit London in the belly with a punch that drove all the smaller man's air out of his body. For several anxious moments he didn't think it would ever come back, then just as the edges of his vision were starting to go fuzzy he was suddenly able to take a breath.

"Did you kill our brother?"

"No."

"Did Clint Adams kill him?"

"No."

"Now why should I believe that?"

"Look, Sykes," London said, "I'm tired of playin' this game."

He stomped on Joe's instep with the heel of his boot. The man bellowed and released his hold on the gambler. London launched a punch that caught Al flush on the jaw. The punch didn't move the big man, who punched London in the same place. London felt something go in his jaw as he tumbled backward.

"I don't know if you killed our brother or not," Al Sykes said, standing over London, "but I know you took his gold."

"He los' it," London said, but the words didn't come out right. His jaw was broken from Al Sykes's punch.

"You took it from him," Sykes said, "and now we're gonna take something from you."

"I din' kill 'im," London said.

"I think he broke my foot!" Joe cried.

"It doesn't matter now whether you killed him or not," Al said.

"I din'. Adams killed 'em."

"Adams?"

"I . . . I swear," London said, hating himself.

"We're gonna need Bannister," Ed said.

"My damn foot—"

"Shut up, Joe," Ed said. "What do we do, Al?"

"First we take care of this tinhorn gambler," Al said, "and then we take care of Adams."

Al reached for London and pulled him to his feet. The gambler's jaw was throbbing, but for a moment he thought he was safe. He hated doing it, but maybe giving them Clint had saved his life.

"What do we do with him?" Ed asked Al.

"Just stand back, boys," Al said. "I'm the head of the family. I'll handle it."

Ed and Joe backed away. London's eyes never left Al's face.

"Wha—" he started, but before he could get another word out Al hit him in the jaw again. The pain was so intense that London blacked out, and didn't feel any of the blows that landed after that.

Clint finished his beer and went up the stairs to his room. Before entering, though, he noticed that the door to London's room was ajar. There was a shaft of light shining out into the hall. He went to the door and pushed it open. London was lying on the floor, a bloody mess. One of his legs was at an odd angle, and when Clint turned him over he could see that damage had been done to his jaw as well.

"London? Can you hear me?"

London's eyes fluttered. He was still alive, but in bad shape.

"Hang on, London," Clint said, "just hang on."

FORTY-ONE

Clint and Virgil Train were in the doctor's office the next morning, standing outside his examination room. Clint had gotten Train first last night, and then had alerted the doctor while Train had some men carry Billy London to the man's office. The doctor had sent them away and told them to come back in the morning. Now they were waiting to hear how much damage had been done to the gambler.

"It was the Sykes brothers," Clint said.

"You don't know that," Train said.

"No, I don't know it, but who else do you think would do this?"

"I think it may be them, yeah," Train said, "but we still don't know."

"Then we'll just have to find them and ask them," Clint said.

"*I'll* ask them, Clint."

"And what do you suggest I do? Just wait for them to come after me next?"

"You look for Newman, like we planned."

Before Clint could argue, the doctor came out, shaking his head.

"Somebody gave that man an amazing beating. It's a miracle he's still alive."

"How bad, Doc?" Train asked.

"He's got a leg that's broken in two places, probably has some broken ribs, and his jaw is definitely broken. He might have some loose teeth, but I can't get his mouth open wide enough to find out. Also, somebody broke all of his fingers."

"All his fingers?" Clint asked.

"Yes."

"Will he recover?" Clint asked.

"He's not going to die, but I don't know how well he's going to recover. He's a gambler, isn't he?"

"That's right."

"I don't think he'll ever be able to shuffle a deck of cards again."

"Can we see him, Doctor?" Clint asked.

"He can't speak."

"I can still ask him yes or no questions, if he's well enough to answer."

"As long as he doesn't have to move much. I'd suggest one of you going in, though."

Clint looked at Train.

"All right," Train said, "you go in."

The doctor opened the door and Clint walked in. London was lying on a table, his leg in a splint. He had a bandage around his head and jaw, tied in a knot on top of his head. The doctor had said there was nothing he could do for the man's broken or cracked ribs. He just had to keep still and let them heal.

"Hello, London," Clint said.

The gambler's eyes opened and he looked up at Clint.

"How are you?"

London raised his eyebrows. They were probably the only thing on him that didn't hurt. His jaw was swollen, as was his mouth. Both of his hands were wrapped.

"I know you can't talk," Clint said, "but we have to have some signal for yes or no. Blink one eye for yes and both for no. Understand?"

London blinked one eye.

"Good. Did the Sykes brothers do this to you?"

One eye blinked.

"All three of them?"

Hesitation, then one eye blinked.

"They must think you killed Harley."

London blinked both eyes.

"No? Who do they think killed him?" Clint realized that wasn't a yes or no question. "Do they think I killed him?"

One eye blinked.

"If they think I killed him, then why did they do this to you? All right, you can't answer that. Maybe it's because we're friends?"

Two eyes.

"Then it must be because you won his gold from him—their gold."

One eye blinked.

"Okay," Clint said, "just rest easy. Doc says . . . you're going to be all right."

London blinked both eyes. He didn't believe that lie for a second.

"Rest," Clint said. "I'll come and see you again. We'll get you moved to your hotel room."

London closed both eyes but didn't open them again. Either it took too much effort, or he had simply fallen asleep.

Clint turned and walked out.

"Well?" Train asked.

"I'll tell you outside."

They left the doctor's office and started walking.

"It was Al Sykes and his brothers."

"They think he killed Harley?"

"He says they think I killed Harley."

"Then why did they give him a beatin'?"

"I'm not sure. Maybe because he kept winning Harley's gold."

"I'll have to find them," Train said.

"I'll go with you."

"No, do as we agreed last night. Find Newman."

"I didn't agree to that," Clint said. "You did."

"Clint, do this my way. If you go after the Sykes boys, somebody's gonna get killed."

"I can't just wait for them to come after me."

"They won't," Train said. "Not if I can help it."

"The question is, can you?"

"What's that mean?"

"It means you don't know what you are, Train. You're wearing a badge and a collar, and the two things just don't go together. I don't feel I can leave my life in your hands."

Train grabbed Clint's arm and stopped walking.

"Don't go up against me, Clint," Train said. "You'll end up in jail or . . ."

"Or what?"

The two men glared at each other. Clint knew Train's reputation with a gun, but he guessed that the man had been out of practice while he took up preaching.

"You don't want to go up against me, Train," he said.

"You're right, Clint," Train said, dropping his hand from Clint's arm, "I don't . . . but I will if you force me to."

Clint looked into the man's eyes and knew that he meant it.

"Damn it—" he said. "All right, Sheriff. You find the Sykes boys, and I'll find Newman."

Train heaved a sigh of relief.

"All right."

"But don't try to take them alone, Virgil," Clint said.

"I don't have a deputy, Clint."

"Find them and talk to them, but don't try to take them without me. Alone, we might each have to kill them. Together, we might be able to bring them in alive."

After a moment Train said, "All right. Agreed."

"Wait a minute," Clint said before they parted company. "They have a cousin named Bannister Smith."

"If you say so. That means there'll be four of them, then."

"Have you ever heard of Bannister Smith?"

"No, should I?"

"He's got a reputation with a gun," Clint said.

"I've lost track of that sort of thing."

"Well, if you come up against him, just watch him. He might be their cousin, and they seem to prefer inflicting damage with their hands, but he'll use a gun."

"I'll keep it in mind," Train said. "Thanks for the warning."

"Train," Clint said as the lawman started walking away.

"Yeah?"

"When's the last time you drew your gun on a man?"

He didn't answer. Instead he just turned and walked away—which was, in itself, an answer.

FORTY-TWO

Clint went back to the saloon and found Vince behind the bar, getting it ready to open.

"You look terrible," he said.

"You don't know the half of it." Clint told Vince what had happened to London the night before.

"Jesus. How bad is he?"

"He'll live, but he's in bad shape." He outlined all of the gambler's injuries, and Vince winced at every one of them.

"How the hell did they get into his room?"

"Must've used the window. It was open."

"You goin' after the Sykes boys?"

"No," Clint said, "the sheriff is looking for them."

"What are you gonna do?"

"I need to find a man named Newman, Vince. Help me out."

"Ben Newman?"

"That's right."

166

"Why do you want him?"

"He was playing poker with us the night Harley Sykes was killed."

"So was Kevin Carpenter, wasn't he?"

"I need to find Newman."

"He's involved in this?"

"I think so. Do you know where he lives?"

Vince hesitated, then said, "Since he lost his claim he's been hanging around the cribs."

"Thanks, Vince."

"Clint, if you don't mind me sayin', Newman's harmless."

"I'll keep that in mind."

Clint turned to leave and saw Jenny coming down the stairs.

"I spent the night in your room," she said. "What happened to you? Are you all right?"

"I am," Clint said, "but London's not." He told her what had happened.

"Where'd you spend the night?"

"I spent it at the doctor's office, and then the sheriff's office."

"You look terrible. You need some sleep."

"There are some things I need to get done, Jenny. I'll see you later."

"You be careful, Clint."

"I will."

He left the saloon again, aware that there was a burning behind his eyes. He was tired, but he was also angry at what had happened to London. Three men the size of the Sykes brothers beating on a man London's size just didn't sit right with him. Three against one in any instance was cowardly.

He didn't think the Sykes boys were cowards, though. Ed and Joe, they were too stupid to be cowards, and Al was just too brutal to worry about it. Clint hoped that Train wouldn't do anything foolish if and when he found them.

As he walked to the end of town where the cribs were, he wondered what part Newman played in all this. How harmless was he if he was trying to set Clint and London against the Sykes brothers? Could he have been the one to kill Harley Sykes as well? And if so, how damned harmless did that make him?

Clint's last question to him angered Train, although he wasn't quite sure why it should have. Should he be ashamed because he hadn't killed a man since he turned to God, that he hadn't even drawn his gun on anyone?

Since Clint Adams's arrival in town he had started questioning the way he lived. Once again, it seemed, he was going to have to make some changes. Give up the badge? The gun? The Lord?

He thought the badge would be the easiest, but between the gun and God he just wasn't all that sure.

FORTY-THREE

The "red-light" end of town was much like that of every other town Clint had ever been in. Everything was cheaper there, but with the cheaper price came more danger—danger of catching a disease from a dirty whore, or of being robbed by her pimp, or even killed.

Clint began stopping at cribs, turning cheap whores down and asking if they knew where Ben Newman was.

"Why are you askin'?" one emaciated whore asked.

"Because it's worth money to me," he said.

"How much?"

"Five dollars?"

"Let's see it."

He took out the money and showed it to her.

"Tent at the end of this row. The girl's name is Brandy, but Newman's in there."

Clint looked that way, wondering if she was lying to him for the five dollars.

"I'm not lyin', mister," she said, as if reading his mind. "I really need the money."

Clint handed her the five dollars.

"Thanks, mister. Do you, uh, wanna come in?"

"No thanks."

He left her standing there in her threadbare robe and walked the way she'd indicated.

It was Bannister Smith who spotted Clint by the cribs and saw him walking to the end. He'd seen the Gunsmith once in his life, but it had left an indelible impression. It was him, all right. Now all he had to do was find his cousins.

When Clint got to the tent at the end he stopped and listened. He heard familiar sounds, a man and a woman together. Rather than call out, he just tossed the tent flap back and entered.

"Hey!" a man shouted.

Clint saw Newman and a thin woman on a pallet, both of them naked. The woman was actually on her knees in front of him. His penis was erect and glistening with saliva, so it wasn't hard to figure out what they had been doing when he interrupted them.

"Tell the woman to take a walk, Newman."

"Wha—Adams!"

"Who is this?" the woman asked. "Newman?"

The man got to his feet and grabbed for his pants, but Clint pulled them away. In his experience a man without pants was usually not much of a danger—

especially if he was also naked and exhibiting what was now a rapidly shrinking erection.

"Tell her to get lost, Newman."

"Get out, Brandy."

"Hey," she said, getting to her feet. She was so thin her ribs and hipbones stood out. To Clint she looked diseased, and he was suddenly uncomfortable being in the tent.

"It's my tent!" she complained.

"Get out, Brandy!" Newman shouted, keeping his eye on Clint's gun.

She grabbed for a robe, put it on, and hurried outside.

"Take it easy, Mr. Adams—" Newman said, holding his hands out.

"You killed Harley Sykes, didn't you, Newman?"

"Wha—me—no—I—"

"Yeah, you did. You saw a perfect opportunity when he threatened us, and you knew when you killed him London and I would be suspected."

"Believe me—"

"I don't. I think you wanted to pit us against the Sykes brothers."

"Why?"

"Because your claim dried up and you want another one," Clint said.

He knew even if this wasn't true that Newman had *something* to tell him. Maybe he'd be scared enough to talk.

"Come on, Newman," Clint said. "Fess up. You did it, didn't you?"

* * *

Bannister Smith found the Sykes brothers and told his cousins that he had seen Clint Adams by the cribs.

"He's lookin' for you," Al said, "or us."

"Why?"

"He killed Harley, Bannister," Al said.

"You know for sure?"

"The gambler told us."

Bannister Smith took his gun out, checked the loads, and said, "Well, maybe we should let him find us."

FORTY-FOUR

"Okay," Newman said, "okay, but gimme my pants, huh?"

"Not until you talk to me."

"I didn't mean to kill him, but . . . but there he was, ya know? And I saw my chance, like you said. I figured his brothers would come after you and you'd kill them easy, with or without the gambler."

"And then you'd step in and take their claim."

"Right."

"Sounds like it was a good plan, Newman."

Newman shook his head and said, "It was crazy. I realized that after I shot him, but what could I do then? It was done, ya know?"

"Yeah, I know," Clint said. He tossed Newman his pants. "Put these on and we'll go talk to the sheriff."

Newman caught the pants and pulled them on, then sat down to put on his boots.

"How about you just let me go, Adams?" he asked.

"I ain't did nothin' to you."

"You set me up to kill three or four men, or be killed by them," Clint said. "I tend to take that sort of thing personally, Newman."

"I didn't mean nothin'," Newman said. "I was just tryin' to get back on my feet."

"Get a shirt on and let's go, Newman," Clint said. "I just want to get this all straightened out."

Newman grabbed his shirt and put it on. Clint looked around for a gun but he couldn't see one.

"Are you ready?"

"Yeah, I guess so," Newman said glumly. "What's this world comin' to when ya can't even try to survive?"

"You don't survive by killing other people," Clint said.

"Why not? That's what you got your reputation for."

"You don't know what you're talkin' about, Newman," Clint said. "Let's go."

Clint allowed Newman to go out of the tent in front of him, which saved his life. . . .

As the Sykes brothers and Bannister Smith approached the last tent, the woman came out and started toward them.

"Hold on," Smith said, "that's Brandy. It's her tent."

He grabbed the woman by the arm and stopped her.

"Where are you off to in such a hurry?"

"There's a crazy man in the tent with Newman,"

she said. "I'm goin' for the sheriff."

"No sheriff," Al said to Smith.

"Forget the sheriff, Brandy," Smith said. He released her arm and said, "Just find someplace where you can lay low for a while."

"But, Bannister—"

"Do as I tell you!"

"All right," she said, rubbing her arm where he had grabbed her.

"Let's go," Al said.

As they approached the tent, the flap opened and a man stepped out.

"It's him!" Ed said, and fired his rifle.

"Damn it, don't—" Al started, but the blast of Joe's shotgun drowned him out.

"Stupid—" Smith said.

"Oh, hell," Al said, and started firing.

Clint heard the shot, and then the shotgun blast. He felt the sting as some of the pellets struck him on the arm and side, but Newman took the brunt of the blast. It threw him back into Clint, who fell to the ground with Newman's body on him. He was about to push the man off when the tent was suddenly riddled with bullets. He remained pinned beneath the dead body for protection.

Sheriff Virgil Train was approaching the cribs when he heard the shots. First what sounded like a rifle, and then the unmistakable blast from a shotgun. After that there was a volley of shots. He drew his gun and ran to see what the hell was going on.

FORTY-FIVE

When the shooting subsided, Clint quickly rolled the body off of him and scrambled to the back of the tent. Bullets had riddled the canvas with holes from front to back. He put his fingers through some of those holes and tore through the back of the tent.

"Adams!" a voice called. He thought he recognized it as Al Sykes. "Come on out, Adams. We know you killed Harley. London told us."

Clint slipped through the tear in the back of the tent and moved into the darkness behind it. Was Sykes telling the truth? Had London given him up as the killer? Given the beating he'd received, Clint wouldn't have been surprised if he had, but he couldn't afford to think about that.

"Come on out, Adams," Sykes said. "Don't make us come in after you."

"Come ahead," Clint called, figuring it would sound like his voice was coming from the tent, "but you already killed the man who killed your brother."

There was a long silence and then Al Sykes called out, "You killed our brother!"

"Ben Newman killed him, Al," Clint said, "and that was Ben Newman you shot coming out of the tent just now."

"The gambler said you did it—"

"That's because you were breaking his fingers at the time, Al," Clint said. "Think about it. He would have said anything to make you stop."

"That's where you're wrong, Adams," Al said, with satisfaction. "He already gave you to us before I started breaking his fingers. Your friend gave you up to save himself."

"I'm not coming out, Al," Clint called. "You'll have to come in after me."

He moved out of the darkness and alongside the tent. He stayed close to the side and moved forward until he could see them. They were across from the tent, standing out in the open, the four of them. Clint assumed the fourth man was Bannister Smith, the cousin. While he watched, it looked like Smith and Al were arguing.

"I told you I wanted to take him myself," Smith said.

"Don't blame me," Al said. "These idiots started firing."

"I only fired after Ed did," Joe said.

"Shut up, Joe," Ed said.

"Was that Ben Newman coming out?" Al asked.

"It looked like him," Smith said, "but I didn't get

much time to take a look at him before Joe cut him in half with the shotgun."

"I only shot after Ed—"

"Shut up, Joe!" Both Al and Ed Sykes had spoken.

"We've got to take Adams together, Bannister," Al said.

"I can take him alone," Smith insisted.

While Bannister Smith was better with a gun than all three Sykes brothers put together, Al didn't seriously think he could take Clint Adams in a fair fight.

"Do it my way, Bannister," Al said. "After all, he was our brother."

"I don't give a damn about Harley, Al," Bannister Smith said. "He was an idiot. I just want my fair chance at Clint Adams."

"He'll kill you, Bannister."

"Maybe," Smith said, "but the way I look at it, I ain't got such a great life, anyway. If I kill him, it'll get better. If he kills me . . ." Smith ended with a fatalistic shrug of his shoulders.

Al Sykes thought it over a few moments and then said, "Go ahead, then. See if he'll go for it."

"Adams?"

A new voice this time.

"This is Bannister Smith. Do you hear me?"

"I hear you," Clint called back, confident that it would still sound like he was in the tent.

"You know me?"

"I've heard of you."

"The others have agreed to make it just you and me. What do you say?"

"I walk away if I kill you."

There was silence and then Smith said, "Yeah, that's right."

Sure, Clint thought. Still, this would be better than facing four of them. After he killed Smith, the Sykes boys would start shooting, and it would be three against one.

"Okay, Smith, you got a deal."

"Step on out, then," Smith said. "Let's do it."

Clint drew his gun, checked his loads, then holstered it, took a deep breath, and stepped out and away from the tent.

FORTY-SIX

Train saw the men standing at the far end of the row of cribs. Four on one side, and one on the other. The lone man was Clint Adams, and it looked as if he had stepped out in the open to face the other four. Did he think he was that good with a gun? Sure, he'd shot three men in the saloon, but their attention had been split between Adams and London. What was he thinking?

Train slowed down as he approached because he didn't want to provoke any sudden action. As he watched, one of the four men separated himself from the other three. It became apparent that this man was going to face Clint Adams alone. The man must have been Bannister Smith.

Train stopped when he came within range and had still not been noticed by the others. The three Sykes brothers were watching the action with interest. Train had no doubt that if Clint killed Bannister Smith, the Sykes boys were ready to kill him.

And he was ready to do his part as well.

It obviously surprised the Sykes brothers and Bannister Smith when Clint did not come from inside the tent but the side of it.

"How the hell—" Joe Sykes started.

"Shut up, Joe," the other three told him.

Bannister Smith stepped away from his cousins as Clint Adams moved around in front of the tent.

"This is an opportunity I never thought I'd get, Adams," Smith said.

Clint wasn't impressed with Smith. He was almost as big as the Sykes boys, he *was* as worn and shaggy-looking, and his gun and gun belt looked aged.

Fanned out behind Smith were the three brothers. Joe and Ed were holding their shotgun and rifle, certainly reloaded by now. Al's pistol was holstered. When Smith went down between them, Clint would be facing those three, with his gun already out. By allowing Smith to face him alone they'd lost a lot of their advantage.

Still, three-to-one odds were always daunting, especially when the gamble was life or death.

"I told you boys you already got Harley's killer," Clint said.

"This ain't about Harley's killer for me, Adams," Smith said.

"Then stop talking, Smith," Clint said, "and do it."

• • •

The action all took place right in front of Train. He saw Bannister Smith go for his gun. He *never* saw Clint go for his, and yet there it was in his hand. He fired once and Smith jerked and went down.

"Get him!" Al Sykes shouted.

Train gauged that the shotgun in Joe's hands was the biggest threat to Clint, so he fired swiftly. Joe stiffened as Train's bullet struck him, then staggered into his brother Ed.

Clint considered the older brother, Al, to be the biggest threat, so when he fired a second time he put a bullet in Al's massive chest before the man had a chance to draw his gun. He killed Ed next, who was thrown off balance by Joe, and then noticed that Joe had already gone down.

Train came walking into the clearing in front of the tent, his gun still in his hand.

"Thanks for the help," Clint said. He ejected the spent shells from his gun and loaded live ones before holstering his gun.

"What the hell happened?" Train asked.

"I found Newman. He's inside. They killed him when we were coming out of the tent. I guess they thought it was me coming out first."

"What did Newman say?"

"He killed Harley, then tried to pit me and London against the Sykes brothers."

"Did you tell that to them?"

"I did, but they didn't want to hear it. They said that London told them I killed Harley."

"Why would he do that?" Train reloaded his spent round and holstered his gun.

"Fear, I guess."

Train shook his head, then looked down at the dead men.

"Bannister Smith wanted to try me first," Clint said, looking down at the man.

"That's where they made their mistake," Train said. "Four against one might have been too much even for you."

"Maybe," Clint said, "but then you would have been here, anyway. Four against two wouldn't have been so bad."

"I guess not. What are you going to do now?"

Clint thought briefly of his bet with Rick Hartman. It didn't seem so important now.

"I guess I'll head out."

"Will you see London?"

Clint shook his head.

"I don't think so. Will you tell him what happened for me?"

"Sure," Train said, "I'll tell him everything."

Clint nodded.

"And what about you, Virgil? What are you going to do?"

"After I've cleaned up this mess, I think I'll turn in my badge."

"Going to stay here?"

"No," Train said, "I think I'll find someplace where they want a preacher, where I can build a church."

"A preacher with a gun?"

Train looked down at his holstered weapon.

"I haven't decided about that yet, Clint," Train said. "Guess I've got some time before I have to make that decision, though."

"I guess you do. I wish you luck, Virgil."

"I'll see you in the morning, before you leave."

"I don't know," Clint said, thinking of the six men he'd killed while he was in Chinaville. "I think I might want to get a real early start."

Watch for

THE FRENCH MODELS

168th in the bold GUNSMITH
series from Jove

Coming in December!

If you enjoyed this book, subscribe now and get...

TWO FREE

A $7.00 VALUE–

If you would like to read more of the very best, most exciting, adventurous, action-packed Westerns being published today, you'll want to subscribe to True Value's Western Home Subscription Service.

Each month the editors of True Value will select the 6 very best Westerns from America's leading publishers for special readers like you. You'll be able to preview these new titles as soon as they are published, *FREE* for ten days with no obligation!

TWO FREE BOOKS

When you subscribe, we'll send you your first month's shipment of the newest and best 6 Westerns for you to preview. With your first shipment, two of these books will be yours as our introductory gift to you absolutely *FREE* (a $7.00 value), regardless of what you decide to do. If you like them, as much as we think you will, keep all six books but pay for just 4 at the low subscriber rate of just $2.75 each. If you decide to return them, keep 2 of the titles as our gift. No obligation.

Special Subscriber Savings

When you become a True Value subscriber you'll save money several ways. First, all regular monthly selections will be billed at the low subscriber price of just $2.75 each. That's at least a savings of $4.50 each month below the publishers price. Second, there is never any shipping, handling or other hidden charges—*Free home delivery*. What's more there is no minimum number of books you must buy, you may return any selection for full credit and you can cancel your subscription at any time. A TRUE VALUE!

A special offer for people who enjoy reading the best 'Westerns published today.

WESTERNS!

NO OBLIGATION

Mail the coupon below

To start your subscription and receive 2 FREE WESTERNS, fill out the coupon below and mail it today. We'll send your first shipment which includes 2 FREE BOOKS as soon as we receive it.

Mail To: **True Value Home Subscription Services, Inc. P.O. Box 5235**
120 Brighton Road, Clifton, New Jersey 07015-5235

YES! I want to start reviewing the very best Westerns being published today. Send me my first shipment of 6 Westerns for me to preview FREE for 10 days. If I decide to keep them, I'll pay for just 4 of the books at the low subscriber price of $2.75 each; a total $11.00 (a $21.00 value). Then each month I'll receive the 6 newest and best Westerns to preview Free for 10 days. If I'm not satisfied I may return them within 10 days and owe nothing. Otherwise I'll be billed at the special low subscriber rate of $2.75 each; a total of $16.50 (at least a $21.00 value) and save $4.50 off the publishers price. There are never any shipping, handling or other hidden charges. I understand I am under no obligation to purchase any number of books and I can cancel my subscription at any time, no questions asked. In any case the 2 FREE books are mine to keep.

Name _____

Street Address _____ Apt. No. _____

City _____ State _____ Zip Code _____

Telephone _____

Signature _____
(if under 18 parent or guardian must sign)

Terms and prices subject to change. Orders subject
to acceptance by True Value Home Subscription
Services, Inc.

11747-1